BECOMING
RUBY

OTHER BOOKS BY KATHY STINSON

YOUNG ADULT FICTION

Fish House Secrets

One Year Commencing

JUVENILE FICTION

Seven Clues In Pebble Creek

The Great Pebble Creek Bike Race

King of the Castle

Marie-Claire: Dark Spring (Our Canadian Girl)

Marie-Claire: A Season of Sorrow (Our Canadian Girl)

NON-FICTION

Writing Picture Books: What Works and What Doesn't

Writing Your Best Picture Book Ever

The Fabulous Ball Book

PICTURE BOOKS

Red Is Best

Big Or Little?

The Bare Naked Book

The Dressed Up Book

Those Green Things

Teddy Rabbit

Who Is Sleeping In Aunty's Bed?

Mom And Dad Don't Live Together Any More

I Feel Different: A Book About Being Adopted
(previously published as *Steven's Baseball Mitt:
A Book About Being Adopted*)

BECOMING RUBY

KATHY STINSON

PENGUIN CANADA

Published by the Penguin Group

Penguin Books, a division of Pearson Canada, 10 Alcorn Avenue, Toronto, Ontario,
Canada M4V 3B2

Penguin Books Ltd, 80 Strand, London WC2R 0RL, England

Penguin Putnam Inc., 375 Hudson Street, New York, New York 10014, U.S.A.

Penguin Books Australia Ltd, 250 Camberwell Road, Camberwell, Victoria 3124, Australia

Penguin Books India (P) Ltd, 11, Community Centre, Panchsheel Park,
New Delhi – 110 017, India

Penguin Books (NZ) Ltd, cnr Rosedale and Airborne Roads, Albany,
Auckland 1310, New Zealand

Penguin Books (South Africa) (Pty) Ltd, 24 Sturdee Avenue, Rosebank 2196, South Africa

Penguin Books Ltd, Registered Offices: 80 Strand, London WC2R 0RL, England

First published 2003

1 3 5 7 9 10 8 6 4 2

Song credits: Happy Together © 1966/1967 Alley Music Corp. Trio Music Co. Inc. BMI;
God Only Knows © 1966 Irving Music Inc. BMI; *Good Vibrations* © 1966 Irving
Music Inc. BMI; *Only Love Can Break A Heart* © 1962 Bacharach/David;
Crying © 1961 Sony.

*Publisher's note: This book is a work of fiction. Names, characters, places and incidents either
are the product of the author's imagination or are used fictitiously, and any resemblance to
actual persons living or dead, events, or locales is entirely coincidental.*

Manufactured in Canada.

NATIONAL LIBRARY OF CANADA CATALOGUING IN PUBLICATION

Stinson, Kathy
Becoming Ruby / Kathy Stinson.

ISBN 0-14-301289-4

I. Title.

PS8587.T56B42 2003   C813'.54   C2003-900004-4
PZ7

Visit Penguin Books' website at **www.penguin.ca**

Dedicated in loving memory to Joyce and Julia

BECOMING
RUBY

CHAPTER
ONE

THE WATER IN FRONT OF OUR COTTAGE is only up to my waist and soupy-warm. Already my feet are sinking into mush and weeds. After the crazy heat of today, I have had it with the shallowness of the water at our place. It's one thing to put up with it on weekends, another to be stuck with it for three whole weeks of holidays.

"Forget this, Susie. I'm going over to the park." I wade toward the shore where the rippled lake-bottom is firm.

"You can't wear that bathing suit over there," Susie says. "Mom says it's not decent."

I tug down the edge of white nylon that keeps riding up my bum. "It's fine."

April stops dog-paddling and crosses her arms like Mom does. "When the top gets wet, you can see your boobies right through."

"Can not."

Even if you can, I figure, who's looking? It's not like there's much of me up there, though I have grown some in the three years since I told Mom I wanted a bra and she said, "Nanny dear, I don't think they make them that small."

Through shin-deep water I wade toward the park. It's late enough in the evening that Mom is doing supper dishes, and Dad and Gary are out on the lake fishing, but it's still warm out.

"Nanny, can I come?" April asks.

"No, it's almost your bedtime. Susie will stay here with you. And April, it's bad enough that Mom calls me Nanny. Can you please call me Nan?"

"Okay, Nan."

April holds her face up out of the water, paddles her cupped hands again and kicks.

"Don't go out too deep," Susie tells her.

"I won't."

She won't either. April is the most obedient child I've ever known. More obedient, even, than Susie.

I wade past the empty lot next door to the park, where banners are already up for next weekend. *Grey Bruce Municipal Regatta 1967.*

Gritty sand on the boards of the L-shaped dock, rough with flaking yellow paint, rubs the soles of my feet. Heat smells linger—suntan lotion and sweat, lake water and damp towels, hot bodies and sweet koolaid. Kids wade in the roped area while their parents pack up picnic blankets and coolers. On the far side of the dock, teenagers dive and jump into the deep water, splashing and whooping. I grab the cool iron ladder and climb to the diving board.

Under the water it's green. Darker as I slice deep. And cooler. Almost cold. I propel myself upward and feel the temperature of the water climb with each stroke of my arms.

I hoist myself back onto the dock and fix the bottom of my suit. The sun is barely high enough in the sky to warm my skin now, as I wait for another turn at the diving board.

Again I dive, and again. My body pierces the water cleanly. My skin tingles. I don't feel like a *Nanny*. I don't even feel like *Nan*. Why am I called by my middle name anyway, when my first name is Ruby? Do I feel more like a Ruby?

Soon all the families at the park have gone home. Only two boys are left, two boys and me jumping together from the side of the dock to see who can make the biggest splash, jump the farthest, stay under the longest. Over at the cottage, Susie and April trot towel-wrapped inside.

I laugh as water runs in sheets down my white suit and tanned body. The boys laugh too—*with* me, not *at* me like the boys at school sometimes do. The air is getting cool. It feels warmer in the water. The boys and I stay under longer between jumps. They follow me when I swim out from the dock. I feel strong—kicking and reaching, stretching and breathing—alive. And beautiful. Swimming with that one boy especially, the dark one with the scar on his shoulder, makes me want . . .

I'm not sure what it is I want.

Back on the dock, droplets of water slide down my body. I shiver. The boy's eyes, the one I like, pass slowly over the swelling of my breasts, the hard bumps of the nipples I know must be showing through my wet suit. He can probably see the nipple shadows too, and lower down my dark triangle. But not what is happening to me inside.

The dock creaks against my push-off. Going deep I remember skinny-dipping earlier this summer, at midnight, when my parents were asleep. I remember how the water felt caressing every inch of my skin, especially my usually covered-up breasts and stomach and between my legs. I imagine doing it—swimming naked with that boy—if only his friend would leave. Would he take off his suit too?

My head splashes up through the surface of the water. Someone is standing at the land end of the dock, arms crossed against the now chill breeze. I blink the water from my eyes so I can see through the dusk.

My mother—damn!

I haul myself up onto the dock. To the dark boy with the scar I mutter, "I've got to go."

"Yeah. See you again maybe?"

"Maybe. Are you coming to the regatta on the weekend?"

"Nanny, get over here!" Mom shouts, and I don't hear the boy's answer.

"Bye," I say, barely a whisper.

When Mom tries to throw a towel around my wet shoulders, I shrug her off. Goose bumps nub my arms and thighs, but I don't care. And I don't care that my suit has again ridden up in the back. I like that boy's eyes on me.

"When I ask you to watch your sisters, I mean *watch your sisters!*" Almost pushing me along the pebbly shore of the empty lot, Mom throws a glance behind us. "And have you no shame? That suit is going in the garbage—tonight." She flicks her cigarette butt—hiss—into the water.

INTO THE STATION WAGON WE PILE, April between Mom and Dad in the front seat, the rest of us in the back. Dad drives along the dirt roads and across the marshland. Mom stares straight ahead. As usual, my parents travel in silence. Gary gives out Travel Bingo cards to himself, me and Susie.

I chuck mine back at him. "I don't want one."

Susie looks at me with eyes that say, like Mom's, 'why do you always have to be so difficult?'

All Gary and Susie have found by the time we pull up in front of Stedman's—it's a short trip—is a railroad crossing and a cow.

"Gary," Dad says, "why don't we go check out the fishing lures while the ladies shop for a bathing suit?"

THE WOODEN FLOORBOARDS CREAK as my mother, Susie, April and I look through the racks of brightly coloured swimsuits. I pull a yellow two-piece off the rack and hold it up to see if I like its black edging. Mom says, with great authority, "You don't want a two-piece, Nanny."

What do you know about what I want? I think. But when my mother uses that tone of voice, there's no point in arguing with her.

"How about this one?" April says. She holds up a pink polka-dot one-piece gathered in little puckers all down the front.

"I don't like pink." April looks so crushed that I quickly add, "Not on me. It would look real nice on you."

"That one won't come in Nanny's size anyway," Mom says, "and you don't need a new suit this time."

"Can't you please not call me that, Mom? I'm not a goat."

A woman working in the store passes by. "All the swimsuits are on sale today," she says. "Fifty to seventy-five percent off. We're clearing out summer things to make room for the Back to School displays."

Already? It's only July.

"Mommy, does that mean I can get a suit too?" April asks. "Can I get the pink dotted one?"

"Yes, I suppose so. As long as it fits."

"Can I try on this?" Susie asks. She holds up the yellow

two-piece with black edging. "Or do I just get Nan's old suit this summer?"

"That suit was a mistake from day one and went from bad to worse. You try on what you'd like."

"How come Susie can get a two-piece and I can't?"

Mom just looks at me as if I'm too stupid for words.

"Nan, what colour do you want?" Susie asks.

"I don't know. Orange is good, or yellow. Maybe red. I also really liked my old suit."

"How about this?" Susie holds out a suit that looks like it has caught fire from the bottom edge. Orange and yellow flames curve up from the leg to the shoulder strap on one side and part of the other. The part not on fire is plain black.

It's way cooler than anything I expect of my conservative sister. I hold it up in front of my body. "Is there a mirror somewhere?"

"Oh, Nanny!" Mom looks like she could be physically ill. "*Nan*, excuse me. That suit . . ." She has to work to come up with a fresh objection. "It's such a loud pattern, you'd be tired of it in a week."

"You said find a one-piece. This is one piece."

"Here, take these to the change room. Try them on and see which one you like."

I assumed that the navy blue and maroon suits Mom was carrying over her arm were suits she was considering for herself. "I don't want a dark colour."

"A dark colour is very practical," Mom insists. "You know what a problem it was keeping that white one clean."

"No, I don't. Besides, this one is half black." I hold up the fiery one. "How much darker can you get?"

"Just try these. Black is not a nice colour for a young girl."

I close the door of the change room. The two suits Mom has given me are horrid. Not just their colour, but the little skirts around the hips too, and the stiff pretend boobs sticking out the front.

In the change room next to mine, Susie and April are chattering happily. I slip off my shorts, pop top and bra, and hang them on a hook.

"Be sure to leave on your underpants, girls," Mom says.

All three of us answer together, "I know."

I stand up straight and look at my reflection in the full-length mirror on the back of the door. There's a hole in the toe of my runner. My legs and arms are thin, and very brown next to my white underpants and untanned skin. My breasts have definitely grown this year. For ages after I hit puberty and my nipples got puffy, it seemed as if that would be it—just two swollen dark spots on a flat white chest. But I like what I see in the mirror now. I'm still smaller than a lot of girls going into grade eleven, but I'd never want to be big like, say, Norma, whose brassiere looks like a horse harness.

My face, I think today, is almost pretty. My nose is kind of freckly but not too big, and my chin isn't pointed like

Sandra's or slanted backwards like Harriet's. My hair is a little too brown to be called blonde, but I like how it's cut this summer: short around the sides, the bangs a good length. Sometimes Mom cuts my bangs way too short so I look like the Dutch boy on the cookie tin.

"How are you doing in there?" Mom calls through the door. "Nan?" she adds, as if to show how co-operative she can be even as she forces on me some god-awful swimsuit.

"Fine." I try not to think how nice I'd look in the fiery one Susie found, and pull on the navy blue one Mom handed me.

How is it possible? It's even worse than I thought it would be. The material is thick, like the brocade my dead Nana used to wear. The neckline is practically up to my chin. Where my boobs are supposed to be are rigid spongy cups, and around the hips is that horrid little skirt. I open the change room door so Mom can see how impossibly ugly this suit truly is.

"That's quite nice," she says.

"I don't like it."

"Is it the navy? Why don't you try the maroon?"

"It's not just the colour. I don't like any of it." I pinch the almost empty cups to show my mother how absurd they are.

"It's a good classic suit and it will still fit you next summer."

"It will fit till I'm as old as you," I mutter.

"What did you say?"

"I won't wear it."

"Then you won't swim."

"Fine."

Mom glares at me. "We don't have time to argue, Nanny. Your father and brother will be waiting. We'll decide which one to take after you get dressed."

I close the change room door as loud as I dare, not quite loud enough to be accused of slamming it. I yank the horrid suit down my body.

Whenever I want to go downtown with my friends or to a party where there will be boys, Mom acts like I'm still some little kid. Why *now* am I suddenly so grown up she expects me to wear this . . . this ugly, old-lady *thing*?

Dressed again, I leave both suits hanging on the hook in the change room and come out glowering.

"You said before that you liked red," Mom says, reaching in for the suits. "Let's get the maroon."

"I told you, I won't wear it."

"It's just different from what you've had before. You'll get used to it."

"Should we see if they sell chastity belts here too?"

"I beg your pardon."

"Nothing."

CHAPTER
TWO

SATURDAY MORNING, the weekend of the regatta, the whole
family watches Susie in her yellow two-piece come fifth in the
nine-year-olds. I haven't swum all week. I'll give up swimming
forever before I'll wear that suit Mom insisted on buying.

Dad says, "You coming, Nan?" My family is heading back
to the cottage.

"Can I just stay and watch some of the other races?" I'm
still hoping to see the boy I swam with the other night.

"Sure, just be sure you're home at ten thirty if you want to
go meet Gramma at the bus."

Dad knows I'll want to go. He knows how glad I am that
Gramma is coming. She's so different from Mom, it's hard to
believe the two of them can be related.

While the tournament organizers get the next swimmers
lined up, I try to find the boy's face—long and thin like he
is—in the crowd. From behind me—"Hi."

It's silly I should feel shyer today, fully dressed, than I did in my too-small, worn-out swimsuit. "Hi."

"Aren't you racing today?" he asks.

"No. Are you?"

"No. My little brother's coming down with something, and we're leaving this morning. My mom wants to get him home."

"Oh."

"But I figured you'd be here and I just wanted to come say that was fun the other night."

"Yeah, it was."

"Too bad about your mom."

"I know."

"But I guess it was getting dark anyhow."

"Yeah."

All around me and the boy, people are cheering, clapping hands, but it's like he and I are in a separate bubble. The swimming race means nothing. The sun is hot on the top of my head. The scar on the boy's shoulder stands out white against his dark tan.

"You can touch it if you want."

"What?"

"My scar. I saw you looking at it."

"Oh. Sorry." I do want to trace my finger along it, the white crescent moon of flesh whiter than winter skin. I want to cover it with my palm and feel the warmth of him. I want to be wet with him again and diving.

"It's okay," he says. "I don't mind."

I look at the boy's eyes then and see that he wants it too. He liked me looking at his scar. He wants me to touch it.

"Oh, here you are!" Gary pushes through the crowd. "Mom sent me to find you. It's time to go meet Gramma's bus. Come on. You were supposed to come back at quarter after ten."

"Ten thirty, Dad said."

"It's okay," the boy with the scar says. "I've got to be going too."

The shortcut to our cottage through the water is cut off by the swimming races. Gary hurries me up through the park. The boy goes that way too, but no one says anything till we get to the road.

"So, if we rent this cottage again this summer, can I come see you?" The boy takes his bike from the stand.

"We're the first cottage over, past the empty lot," I tell him. But rental cottages get booked months in advance around here, so I probably won't see him again.

As we hurry down our driveway, Gary says, "Who was that?"

"Just . . . somebody."

IF I HADN'T SAID I WANTED TO GO meet Gramma's bus, I could have stayed longer with the boy. Long enough to find out his name. Long enough, maybe, to touch him. But I do want to be there when Gramma arrives. Problems never seem as big when she's around. She might even know what I'm supposed to do about the ugly swimsuit.

When Gramma steps down off the bus in her flowery sun-dress, Dad takes her suitcase, gives her a kiss and steps aside as she looks around him for her grandchildren.

"April and Susie are helping Mom make lunch," I tell her.

"Nan," Gramma says, embracing me, "don't you look fetching in that orange top. Dressing up for some young man today, I'll betcha."

Why is it when Gramma knows things about me it feels so good? If Mom seems even close to knowing something, it just feels dangerous.

"Gary, bend down here and let your old gramma give you a hug. Being bigger than me doesn't mean you're too big for hugs, you know."

Gary smiles and wraps his gawky arms around her.

"You, too, young man." She reaches up toward Dad.

How did a huggy person like Gramma end up with such an unhuggy daughter?

Gary and Dad get into the front seat of the station wagon. Gramma and I get in the back. When we get going, air from outside blows hot all around us and creates enough noise inside the car to muffle our separate conversations.

"Do you want to tell me what's bothering you?" Gramma asks. "Not boy troubles, I hope."

"No. But how did you know something was bothering me?"

"I've been around a long time. Some things you get good at after a while."

I tell her about having to get a new swimsuit and Mom's insisting on buying one I hate. "I know my old one probably showed more than it should, but there was this really cool one at the store, and Mom just said, 'Oh, Nanny, you won't like that one for long.'"

"Have you worn the new one your Mom bought yet?"

"I'll never wear it, Gramma. I'd swim naked in front of the whole world before I'd wear it, it's that ugly."

"Where did you see this other suit?"

"Stedman's."

"Ted—" Gramma leans forward and taps Dad on the shoulder. "Would you mind making a stop? There's one or two things I need to pick up at Stedman's."

She doesn't mean—could she—that she's going to buy me the other suit?

When Dad pulls up in front of the store, Gramma says, "I'm sorry to take you out of your way, but I won't be long. Nan, would you come with me, please?"

Gramma pushes open the door into the old department store. "Now," she says, "where are the swimsuits?"

"They're on sale, so the one I liked might not still be here." I lead Gramma past socks and underwear. "Even if it is, won't Mom get mad anyway?"

"Your mother has been angry with me before, and she'll no doubt be angry with me again."

It's like when I was little and Gramma took me downtown to the store where she worked. After we wandered aisles full of toys and books and games, and rode the escalators from one floor to another, we spent a long time admiring the rows of girls' dresses, and then she bought me the one I liked best. It was royal blue with blocks of red, yellow, and green threads mixed in. It had a white collar edged with lace, puffed sleeves, and in the back, buttons and a bow. At the cashier counter I suddenly remembered, and told Gramma, "Mommy doesn't like dresses that button in the back."

And she said, "Then it's good this isn't for her, isn't it?"

The fiery-patterned swimsuit I liked is still there. When Gramma sees it, her eyes open wide. Maybe she's going to make me pick another one. But that's okay. Anything will be better than what's sitting in its bag back at the cottage.

"Go try it on, quickly," she says.

Its straps cross in the back, it has an extra layer of fabric in the top instead of spongy cups like the other one, and the pattern of flames curving up the front looks really good on me.

Gramma asks through the door, "Does it fit?"

"Yes."

"Let me see."

When I open the change room door, Gramma nods. "It's beautiful. *You're* beautiful, Nan."

We climb into the car, Gramma clutching the brown paper Stedman's bag in front of her.

"Get what you needed?"

"Yes, thank you, Ted."

"Thank you, Gramma," I whisper.

Dad pulls into the town traffic and soon we're on the dirt road to the cottage. The car bounces down our long bumpy driveway, past the tall pines and into the clearing around the cottage. Mom, standing at the back door smoking, steps outside. "Where have you been? I was starting to worry."

Dad says, "We stopped at Stedman's for your mother."

"But not for more than ten minutes," I add.

"Come inside. Lunch is ready."

Everyone gathers at the round table in front of the big picture window that looks out over the lake. We dive into the plate of sandwiches Mom has made. The choice is peanut butter and lettuce or cheese and tomato. All through lunch no one mentions Stedman's or Gramma's purchase.

After Susie and I have done the dishes, Susie says, "Can we go swimming now?"

"It's not an hour yet," Mom says.

"Didn't dishes take an hour?" Susie complains.

"More like ten minutes," Gary says, leaning over a jigsaw puzzle of a man kayaking through white water.

"Can we just put our suits on then?" April pleads.

"Why don't you girls all go put on your new suits," Mom says. "I'm sure Gramma would like to see them." She lights a cigarette from the end of the one she's just finished.

How can she just sit there and pretend we haven't been waging war over the suit she bought me, pretend I haven't flatly refused to wear the thing—ever?

Dad calls Gary outside to help him with something in the boathouse. April's heels pound the linoleum as she runs to the bedroom; the noise makes her sound twice as big as she is. Susie goes more slowly, no doubt keen to hear the next battle between me and Mom. I look to Gramma, casually getting a paperback book from her purse. "Yes, Nan," she says, making no move to get the bag she put in her room before lunch. "Let's see your new suit."

I don't want to put on the hideous suit, even for a minute. How can Gramma let me down like this? Shoulders heavy, I start to turn toward the bedroom I share with my sisters, and Gramma winks.

In the crowded bedroom, April pokes her feet through the leg holes of her new suit.

"What are you going to do, Nan?" Susie says. "Are you going to put your suit on to show Gramma?"

I sit on the edge of my bed, across from her. "Yeah, I might as well."

"But—"

"It's okay. It'll be okay."

"How?"

"You'll see."

April pulls the straps of her suit up over her shoulders and jumps up on the bed so she can see herself in our small mirror.

"It's cute, April," I say.

"I know." April plunks down beside me. "Too bad yours isn't."

I grab April and kiss her. "Go show Gramma now, 'kay?"

April thumps out of our room. Susie wants to ask me something, but I cut her off. "You too. Go ahead. I'll be out in a minute."

Gramma exclaims over the lovely shade of pink polka-dots on April's suit and the smart trim on Susie's. What, I wonder, is she going to say about mine? *That heavy maroon fabric is simply divine.*

Stepping into the living room I can feel, in the angle of Mom's shoulders and chin, her smug pleasure in her victory.

When Gramma looks up from her book, she doesn't say anything. She laughs. She lays her eyes on me and laughs until she has to hold her sides and tears are rolling down her cheeks.

"April and Susie," Mom says, "you go on outside."

When finally Gramma is able to stop laughing, she dries her face and says, "Heavens to Betsy, Joan, where on earth did you find that thing? Nan, go. Please. Go into my room and change."

"What do you mean," Mom asks as I leave the room, "—change?"

The walls of the cottage don't go right to the ceiling. I can still hear, inside Gramma's bedroom, what is being said on the other side of the closed door.

"When we went to Stedman's, I bought Nan the suit she wanted."

I slip quickly out of the spongy maroon. Perhaps later I can find somewhere to give it a decent burial.

"You didn't buy that awful, flamey-looking one!"

I take the awful, flamey-looking suit out of the bag.

"Nan is growing up, Joan. You have to start letting her make her own decisions."

"I don't . . . know if that's such a good idea. Her judgement sometimes leaves a lot to be desired."

In the mirror of Gramma's dresser, I admire the crossover straps in the back of my new suit and the lick of flames up the front.

"You know, I thought Nan might be exaggerating when she told me how bad the suit you bought was. I thought maybe she hated it simply because you had chosen it. But honestly, Joan, that thing looks like something out of the fat-girl or old-lady department. What were you thinking of, wanting to wrap her up in that?"

Mom doesn't answer.

"Never mind," Gramma says. "I know what you were thinking."

"You don't know me, Mother. You never have."

"It won't work, Joan. Whether you're ready for it or not, that girl is growing up. And she *won't* always make good decisions. Who does? But the only way anyone learns is by making a few bad ones."

Mom answers sharply, "Some bad decisions you have to live with your whole life. I don't want that for Nanny . . . Nan."

Gramma's tone softens but she is still firm. "You have to let her live her life."

In the silence that follows, I know Mom is drawing hard on her cigarette. I can almost hear, after, the soft parting of her lips, a cross between a puff and a pop, as she blows the smoke out the side of her mouth.

When again I step out of the bedroom, I glance at Mom quickly. I'm afraid to look her in the eye, but she is fiddling with her cigarette package. She doesn't want, it seems, to look at me either. Gramma gives me a slight nod, and I scurry outside.

CHAPTER
THREE

AFTER A LONG WEEKEND of rummy, pancakes for breakfast, cheering for boat races, and a game of Monopoly that
everybody except April plays and Gary wins, we take
Gramma to the bus back home.

"Can't you stay for longer?" Gary begs her.

"For tonight's fireworks?" I add.

But Gramma has to go to work the next day, and she
wants to get to bed early; she's been feeling a little tired. We
wave at her bus till it disappears around the corner, out to
the highway.

After supper Dad grabs a life-jacket from a hook by the
cottage door. "I'm going to get a newspaper," he says.
"Anyone feel like coming for the ride?"

I put down the *Teen Beat* magazine I've been reading.
Mom says fifteen is too young for *Seventeen,* but honestly,
I'm almost sixteen. "Can I row, Dad?"

"Sure. And I'd love your company."

"What about the firecrackers?" Susie asks.

"It won't be dark for a while yet. We'll be back in time."

"We'll need bread and milk too," Mom says.

"'Kay." I grab my life-jacket and follow Dad outside, letting the screen door slam behind me. I run down the lawn and jump from the dock into the boat.

"Actually," Mom calls from the doorway, "I think I'd like to go to the store too."

I stop, my arms half into my jacket. If Mom insists on coming, we won't be taking the boat.

"Do you mind, honey?"

After much discussion, as if everyone doesn't already know how it will turn out, the whole family strolls together along the gravel road. Gary shambles ahead as if he isn't with the rest of us. Through trees, between cottages, a rowboat floats by on the lake. A boy trails his fishing line out the back as his father rows.

"Remember when we went fishing, Dad," I say, "that time Gary was away at Wayne's?"

"Nan, don't scuff," Mom says. "Pick up your feet."

"I wasn't scuffing. And April's doing it too."

"April, come walk with Mommy."

Susie's already walking with Mom. Good little Susie.

"Hey, Nan," Gary says, "race you to the *Lots For Sale* sign."

The sun is still high and the evening air hot. Sweat sticks

to my back as I run. Dust flies up from under our feet. A stitch crimps my side as we round the bend past the trailer sites. Gary beats me by a hair.

On the steps of the store, a girl with long blonde hair drapes her legs across her lanky boyfriend's lap and wraps her arms around his neck. She takes a bite from the ice cream sandwich he's holding in the hand that's not on her thigh. He takes a bite, then she does, and between bites, they kiss. Sticky little pecks I pretend not to notice as I trail behind my family up the steps.

The screen door squeaks, then bangs shut behind us. I steal one more peek at the couple outside. The boy's hand is sliding up the girl's thigh. I touch the fine hairs on my own leg.

The fan in the corner barely stirs the muggy air. "Someone better tell that girl," Mom says, "a boy does not buy the cow if he can get the milk for free."

"Are there cows for sale here?" April asks.

"What's Mom so mad about?" I mutter to Gary. "She doesn't even know those people."

Gary shrugs. "She's always mad."

While my parents get what they need, April squeezes four loaves of bread then takes one to the counter. Gary flips through comics, and Susie and I study the waxy lips in the candy display. I puff my own lips bigger for the reflection in the glass.

"Feels like a night for a pop," Dad says. "What's anybody think?" He lifts the heavy lid of the big metal chest.

I hang my face over the chill air. Like a dive into deep water, it cools. Inside the chest, row upon row of exotic caps offer choices. Mountain Dew. Cream Soda. Orange Crush. Root Beer. Tahiti Treat.

"What would you like, Nan?"

"I think I'll have Cream Soda."

"Cream Soda!" Mom says it as if no one in their right mind would choose such a drink. "I thought you liked Orange Crush."

"I do. I just want to try something else this time. Is there something *wrong* with that?"

When we go outside with our pops—Susie and April both have Orange Crush—the couple on the step is gone. After the muggy closeness of the store, the air outside feels cooler. I can feel the sweat on my back drying as I sit in a baked patch of grass away from the rest of my family.

Against my palm the glass bottle is cold. Beads of sweat have formed all over it. I run my finger down its side and dab the drips across my forehead. When I hold the bottle to my eye, the clear red drink inside looks like a giant ruby. My name—Ruby. I slide the cold bottle down my hot face. Mom didn't want me to be Ruby, Dad did; it was his grandmother's name and he liked it. And since Gary's middle name was given to honour some relation of hers, Mom could hardly argue. Nan Ruby Larkin had lousy rhythm, so I ended up Ruby Nan Larkin. But called Nan.

With the cream soda bottle's opening under my nose, I breathe in. The drink's fruity sweetness then the glass neck against my lips feel full of promise. I tip the bottle. Holding the liquid in my mouth, I let it slide over and under my tongue. Its ticklish fizz hits the roof of my mouth. The taste is like a circus, like flying in a balloon. I can push the sweet head right through my nose and breathe it back in again. Ruby.

At last, when my first mouthful of cream soda is warmed and flattened by heat, I swallow. The taste is still there, softly, inside my mouth and down my throat. The next mouthful I swallow right down. Cold and fizzy. And the next. If I drink too slowly, Mom will say to Dad, *See. I told you she wouldn't like it,* like she did when I was little and tried Poppa's Coke and didn't like it because when I burped after, it was like bumblebees inside my nose.

Dad returns the bottles for the refund and we start back along the road. Again, Gary shambles on ahead. His shoulders are broader than I've noticed before. Maybe I haven't really looked at him in a while. Susie helps April pick wildflowers from the side of the road; they're making a bouquet, but the stems of the ones April likes best are too tough, so they drop the others in the ditch and skip to catch up. I run on up the road. A little ahead of my parents and sisters, I turn and announce, "I want you to call me Ruby."

Mom looks as if I've just said I want to be called Scab or Diarrhoea.

Dad smiles. "I've always liked that name."

Gary, close enough to hear my announcement, says, "You don't want to be Nan any more?"

"No. I don't."

Gary looks at me like he's trying to figure out if I'm just trying to make trouble or what.

Mom hands Dad the bag of groceries and lights a cigarette. She blows out a mouthful of smoke. "It's a difficult thing to change your name," she says.

"I'm not changing it. I just want to be called by my other name. My first name."

"Well, you can't expect everyone to suddenly start calling you Ruby when they've been calling you Nan all your life."

"You haven't been calling me Nan all my life; you've been calling me Nanny."

"Ruby's pretty," April says. "I wish my name was Ruby."

"April is pretty too," Mom says. "And so is Nan."

As obnoxiously as I know how, I yell, "Nan ban can fan man pan ran tan van. Nanny bananny canny fanny—"

"Nan, stop it!"

All the rest of the way back to the cottage, I say no more about being Ruby but behave in a way that's impossible for

Mom to find fault with. I walk tall, lift my feet, don't kick at loose gravel, and I keep to the left side of the road.

But my name *is* Ruby.

And Ruby likes cream soda.

CHAPTER
FOUR

FROM UP AND DOWN THE ROAD families are gathering in
the park for the civic holiday fireworks display. We live so
close we don't go over till it's almost dark. I know the boy I
swam with has gone home, but in the crowd near the dock I
find myself looking for him anyway. Something about the
way his lip turned up at one side, the way one eye creased in
the corner when he smiled . . .

Into the black sky hiss the first spurts of colour. Red
streaks, green and blue, explode into gigantic chrysanthe-
mums and reflect double on the water.

"Ooooh!" the crowd says. "Aaaah!"

On the back of the lifeguard chair, where I've never actually seen a lifeguard, my favourite firecracker spins faster
and faster, spraying circles of sparkling colour through the
night—yellow, red, green.

"Ooooh!"

When its dizzy sizzling pattern hisses quietly black, a couple of men from the Cottagers' Association come around to give sparklers to all the kids.

"It's spitting," April says, and quickly hands hers to Dad. Beside me, Susie scribbles orange lines against the black air.

"Look, Susie," I say. "I can spell my name." In swirly lines I write it—*Ruby*.

Gary nudges me with his elbow. "Look." He swirls his sparkler to spell *fuck*.

I make sure Mom isn't watching, and with the hissing point of my sparkler, I copy Gary's word over and over—*fuckfuckfuckfuck*.

I remember the first time I ever heard this wonderful word. I must have been eight or nine. Mom left Gary in charge of me when she was taking baked goods or something over to the church. We had started a game of Chinese checkers, and I was sliding a spare marble around in my mouth when Gary's friend Wayne came to the door. Wayne and a boy named Bruce, who went to a different school. Gary sounded so proud when he said he couldn't go to the ravine with them because he was minding me. But I'd wondered what it was like, the wild wooded place I'd often passed but always with Mom, always holding the side of Susie's carriage or stroller. I wanted to go.

So Gary held my hand and we ran behind his friends. As we crossed the hot field to the edge of the trees, long grass scratched my legs. Bruce led the way along a fallen tree trunk over a creek that ran, barely a trickle, through the weed-choked gulley. Behind him Wayne swung his arms to catch his balance. Bruce yelled, "Watch where the fuck you go grabbing me, you faggot dick-head."

"Faggot faggot faggot," I remember whispering into the crook of my elbow. "Fuck fuck fuck fuck fuck." I didn't know what the words meant, but they felt exciting, like that over-grown place. Like balancing high on the log like a bridge across the creek, held steady by my brother's weight.

I scribble *fuckfuckfuckfuck*, hot and big and swooping across the night sky, till the sparks stop flying and the white glow fades to red, then orange, and disappears to black. My family saunters together back to the cottage.

It's probably not just because of *fuck* that I remember so well that muggy day with Gary and his friends. They'd brought beer there with them too, as I discovered when I followed Gary through a thicket of bushes to a little clearing of flattened grass, and his friends sat up to make room for us. I didn't know then what beer was, only that I'd seen a look on Mom's face once, around brown bottles like the ones Gary's friends had, that told me what was in them was bad. But they belonged, I thought, in this place with the scratchy grass and the tall trees, the bushes so thick you couldn't see out and could only barely hear the cars passing by on the streets above.

Bruce tipped a brown bottle to his lips, and I watched the big lump of his throat as he swallowed.

Of course, I wanted to try some. Gary said no, but settling me into his lap Bruce said, "Come on, Gar. Just a sip." Wayne burped and laughed.

The neck of the bottle was smooth on my lips, like the extra Chinese checker marble. It gave me the same tingle in my belly I got playing doctor behind the garage with the boy next door.

Then Bruce was pushing the bottle harder into my mouth. I didn't like it, the sour taste of what was in it. I didn't like how long and hard his fingers were around my middle.

I didn't say anything, but Gary was right there. "I said NO, Bruce." He pulled the bottle out of my mouth and yanked me up out of Bruce's lap.

"Oh, man," I heard Wayne say as Gary pulled me through the bushes to the path, "does this stuff make you have to piss or what?"

Following my brother down the dark driveway to our cottage after the fireworks, it occurs to me that he has stopped being my hero. At some point—I'm not sure when—he stopped being my hero and started seeming more like a stranger.

ONE EVENING LATER THAT WEEK, Susie and April have gone to bed and Gary is out on the lake fishing with my dad.

Mom is reading a book in the chair in the corner. The pink undersides of the clouds are deepening to red and reflecting with layers of mauve on the smooth surface of the lake. It's the first time I've been alone with Mom since the new bathing suit.

"Sunset's going to be nice tonight," I say.

"Mhm," Mom says without looking up from her book.

"What's that saying about red sky at night? I can never remember which is supposed to be good, a red sky in the morning or at the end of the day."

"Red sky at night, sailors delight. Red sky at morning, sailors take warning."

"You know all those sayings."

"What sayings?"

"You know, about a sow's ear and birds in the bush—stuff like that."

"Logical consequences are the scarecrows of fools and the beacons of wise men."

Staring out the big window I sigh. I wish we could really talk. Like my friend Patty and her mom. They talk about stuff on the news, things they like doing, family stories, stuff that matters. I turn to face my mother.

"What are you reading, Mom?"

"Just a library book." She slips it down the side of the chair, takes a cigarette out of her pack and lights it. "Are you feeling a bit at loose ends tonight?"

"Sort of, I guess."

"We could do something if you'd like."

I shrug. "Like what?"

"Where's that colouring book I bought?" Mom rummages through the magazines and activity books on the shelf under the window.

Again I hear myself sigh. Doesn't my mother know I'm too old for colouring books? Just because I'll sometimes colour with April . . . Sure, the one she's looking for has way more complicated pictures than the ones she buys for my sisters, but . . . Maybe it's that poster I did with Patty for school last year that makes her think I like colouring. Still, you'd think she'd know there's a difference.

"Here it is." Mom puts the book on the round table in front of the window and opens a tin box of pencil crayons. "You pick the page you want to do."

As Mom rearranges the pencil crayons so the points are all facing the same way in the box, I flip through the pages, as if it makes any difference whether we fill in the empty spaces of a mountain landscape or a city garden, a street scene or a harbour. I have a feeling this is one of those things that makes Mom think we're closer than most mothers and daughters—the fact we can sit in the evenings at the cottage and quietly colour together.

My parents, I've noticed, spend a lot of evenings at home quietly. Does Dad sometimes wish they could talk about real things too? Yeah, sure, Ruby. They're married, for crying out loud. They do things in bed together you don't even want to think about. If they have things to talk about, they talk. Just because you're scared to talk to her doesn't mean everybody else is.

"How about this one?" A picture of a storefront with a woman and a bunch of partially dressed mannequins in the window.

The funny thing about this colouring book is that on both sides of each spread is the same picture. One has numbers printed in all the spaces, the other doesn't. Mom has clipped out the colour-by-number chart from the back cover so we can refer to it without having to flip back and forth. I've never bothered to point out that you don't *have* to use the colours suggested by the numbers, so of course we always end up with identical pictures.

"Mom, you take the side without numbers this time," I say, as if it matters.

"Oh, I don't mind. Wouldn't you rather have the clean side?"

"There's not much point switching places now."

Mom takes #1 Poppy Red out of the box and starts to fill in all the shapes that correspond with the shapes marked #1 on my page. I start with #24 Black. We'll work our way through all the pencil crayons, each of us from our end of the row.

I feel like filling in #1 spaces with my #24 pencil, but that won't help if I'm going to try to talk to my mother tonight, so I colour the skirt and Cleopatra-style hairdo on one of the mannequins black.

"Nan, could you please pass the pencil sharpener?" Mom sets a freshly lit cigarette in the ashtray.

Maybe I should just blurt out what I want to say. *I've been thinking . . .* But how to say it? And what is it I want to say exactly anyway? Is she mad about something besides the bathing suit Gramma bought me? How come she smokes so much? Does she ever think about quitting? Or—why won't she call me Ruby? But these questions all sound like the beginning of arguments. I don't want to argue tonight. Just . . . talk.

The little metal edge of the sharpener scrapes shavings off pencil #2 Lemon Yellow. I try to formulate a sentence that might start a real conversation. I don't feel like I know my mother at all, even though I've known her my whole life. Maybe I could ask her what she was like when she was my age. Or how it feels to have a son taller than she is. Or why she married my dad.

What I'd really ask her if I could is—*Mom, why don't you like me?*

Of course I can't ask that. But it doesn't matter how safe a question I ask or how innocent a comment I make. Unless I talk about something like grocery store coupons or the weather, my words will land like a smelly dead fish in the middle of the table. My mother will whisk it into the garbage, wipe away any slime it leaves behind, and pretend the words have never been spoken.

Won't they? Won't she? What makes me so sure?

Because she never talks to me about anything that matters, that's why. And because once when I was little, one day when she looked sad, I asked her if something was the matter because I thought maybe I could make her feel better if I knew what was wrong. But she just said, 'No, and I wouldn't tell *you*, Nanny, even if there was.' Maybe she just meant I was too little to understand, but it didn't feel like that.

Outside the window of the cottage, only a tiny sliver of red on the horizon separates the black water and black sky. I colour in the outside wall of the store with #18 Burnt Sienna. Mom is up to #5 Sapphire Blue. Smoke rises from her cigarette, resting in the ashtray on the table between us.

"Mom . . . ?" I keep my pencil moving on the paper. "Do you ever think about . . ."

Footsteps on the porch, accompanied by upbeat voices.

The tip of my pencil crayon breaks against the page.

Gary drops a big fish on the plastic tablecloth. It smells and its gills are still moving.

CHAPTER
FIVE

THE NEXT NIGHT IT'S HOT, even after supper. Something thuds against the end of the porch I'm painting. I look up. Crossing the empty lot between the cottage and the park is the boy with the scar.

Why now, when I'm in Dad's ratty old work-shirt? Why did he have to come now?

He bends to pick up the soccer ball that has rebounded back to him. Paint drips from my brush. His tan is even darker now than it was the night we swam at the park.

"I thought that was you over here," he says. "How are you?"

"Okay. I'm painting the porch."

"I see that."

"You . . ." I tuck a strand of hair behind my ear and realize I've probably smeared paint across my forehead. "I didn't think you'd be back."

"The owner of the cottage my parents rent had a cancellation." He bounces the ball back and forth between his hands. "Guess you don't want to go swimming, eh?"

"I have a new bathing suit." And oh to be swimming with this boy again, diving deep and kicking and breast-stroking together back up to the light, jumping, splashing and shivering on the dock but not feeling the slightest bit cold. "But I have to finish this."

"Yeah, I thought so." He tucks the ball into the crook of his arm.

He can't leave now. If he does, I may never see him again. The most beautiful boy I have met in my entire life. I didn't realize till tonight, seeing him, how much I have been hoping he would be back. But if he goes again this time, I just know he'll be really gone. All because of this stupid porch.

Brushing a wisp of hair off my forehead, I accidentally smear more paint onto my face. *I have a new bathing suit.* What a stupid thing to say. Oh why did he have to come when I'm *painting*? And why can't I be smart enough to figure out a way to keep him here?

The boy turns toward the park. He is going. With the brush still clenched in my fist, I slap a blob of grey paint on the porch.

"Hey," he says turning back, "can I come see you tomorrow?"

I hope I'm not actually grinning but it feels like I am, and my face always does what it wants. "That'd be great." Patty would tell me I should say, 'If you *want* to,' as if I was a little bored. Play hard to get, she always says, but I'm no good at that stuff.

"What's your name anyway?" the boy asks.

"Um—Ruby." Thank goodness he didn't ask the night we swam, when it was still splodgy old *Nan*.

"Ruby." It sounds almost sexy when he says it. "I'm Daniel."

A beautiful name. Daniel should never be shortened to Dan, and why would anybody ruin it by making it Danny? "Daniel," I say, and we both laugh.

His friends are yelling at him to bring back the ball, and I have to finish the porch, but I will see him tomorrow. Daniel. The boy with the crescent moon of a scar on his dark shoulder. He wants to see me again.

IN THE MORNING he doesn't come. He still hasn't come by the time we're having lunch at the round table in front of the window. After dishes, I take a book outside, lay my towel on the dock, and stretch out in my new bathing suit. If he liked me in my old suit, he'll love me in this one, with its flames licking up the front. If he comes.

It's almost two o'clock. There are lots of people at the park now. Why hasn't he come?

In the water beside me, Susie and April are splashing around with their pink and turquoise floating mattresses. I turn away from the park to say, "Do you two have to play right here?"

"Where else are we supposed to play?" Susie asks.

"How about the moon." I feel a fly crawling on my foot and try to kick it off.

"Hey, want to go to the store?" The fly is Daniel—trickling water from his fingers to my ankle. "We can walk through the water along the shore."

He came.

He said he would come and he did.

"I just have to check with my mom first."

"Can we come?" Susie asks.

"No."

Mom is smoking and doing a crossword puzzle at the table.

"Can I go to the store?" Casual. If she knows how much I want to, she won't let me.

She looks dubious. "Who's the boy?"

"Daniel. Do you need more cigarettes or anything? I could get them if you want."

She hesitates, then says, "Put on your terry cover-up." She reaches into the purse on the back of her chair and hands me a two dollar bill. "Get me one pack and bring back the change."

I tuck the money into the little inside pocket of my terry jacket, which I'm not actually sorry to be wearing. Again, I feel more self-conscious with Daniel than I did the night I met him at the park in the old, almost see-through bathing suit that kept creeping up my bum. Maybe because then we just happened to be swimming together. Today Daniel came to see me on purpose. And today he's got a shirt on. A pale green golf shirt.

"Do you golf?" I ask him as we start along the shore.

"No. Do you?"

"No."

Past the tiny A-frame next door, past the row of cottages high up from the water, we wade along the waterfront, soft waves lapping at our shins. The sun is warm. When we pass a long beach shared by a group of cottages, Daniel says, "We're in the yellow one with the blue trim." He waves to two younger boys building a sand castle far up the beach. "My brothers," he explains.

"You're the oldest?"

"No. I have two more brothers who are older. They've left home. Are the little girls I saw at your place your only sisters?"

"Yeah, but I have an older brother too. You met him at the park that morning."

"He's very protective of you." There's no judgement in what he says, just observation.

As we continue to stroll along the shoreline, it starts getting easier to talk. Daniel doesn't try to be funny, so I don't have to pretend I think he is, or try to be witty myself so he doesn't think I'm boring. And it doesn't seem to matter whether we're talking or not, like it does with most boys.

I ask Daniel, "Where do you usually live?"

He names a town quite a bit north of where I live. He's going into grade eleven. So am I, and we both like English and History better than Science.

"Hey, Ruby, stop a sec." He steps in front of me in the shallow water. "Look at me."

My feet settle into the sandy lake bottom. I look up at Daniel—please don't tell me I have a booger—past his chest and shoulders, and stop at the part of his lip that turns up a little at the corner.

"Let me see your eyes."

If I had pockets, I would shove my hands inside them. I raise my eyes and swallow. He can't be going to kiss me here. There are families playing in the water behind and in front of us. But if he wanted to, I know I wouldn't stop him.

"Hazel," Daniel says. "'Kay, thanks." He starts wading along the shore again, his hands tucked into his pockets.

"What do you mean—hazel?" I pull my feet from the wet sand settling around my ankles.

"The colour of your eyes. I wanted to know."

"No one's ever called my eyes *hazel* before. I thought they were just grey."

"Partly, but you have other colours there too—that makes them hazel."

I'll have to look at my eyes more carefully next time I'm near a mirror.

Far out on the lake, a motor boat putts slowly along. "What colour are *your* eyes?" I ask, hoping we can get face to face again.

"Brown."

At the store, we step out of the water onto the dock and follow the dry sandy path up the grassy hill. Puffs of dust stick to our bare feet.

A poster in the store window says there's a dance tonight in the rec hall next door. "Want to go?" Daniel asks.

"Me?"

He smiles. "Who else?"

"Sure!"

Of course, getting Mom to agree is another question, which I try not to worry about as we wander along the dirt road that winds back to my place, sucking layers of colour off blackballs Daniel bought, checking every few minutes to see if they're yellow, green, blue or pink.

"You have a bit of black," Daniel says when we're almost there. With his finger, he touches the corner of my mouth.

I can't tell if I'm in more of a spin because he touched me

or because I don't know how long I've had candy stuck to my face. I turn away and try to lick it off.

"Don't worry," he says. "I got it."

Daniel comes with me past the stand of white pines and down the driveway to the cottage. We rinse our feet in the bucket by the back door, dry them off and go inside.

As soon as I see Mom, I remember the money tucked in my pocket.

"Mom, I forgot your cigarettes!" She'll never let me go to the dance now, if there was ever any chance she would. "I'm sorry," I say, giving back her money. "I just forgot."

"That's all right," she says. "I have enough to do me till tomorrow." She puts out the cigarette she is smoking. "Are you going to introduce your friend?"

Daniel is standing in our kitchen, his feet big and bare, his hands clasped behind his back. I introduce him to my parents, and he mentions the dance he'd like to take me to. I can see in Mom's face she's about to say no, but before she does, Daniel says, "I can have her home by eleven, Mrs. Larkin."

Mom swallows the objection that was sitting on her lips. "All right." She turns to Dad. "That sounds all right, do you think, Ted?"

I can go. To the dance at the rec hall with Daniel. I can go!

Behind the cottage, I say to Daniel, "How did you know to say that?"

"Say what?"

"About getting me home by eleven. She was going to say no, I know it, but you said exactly the right thing."

Daniel smiles and shrugs. "Just lucky I guess." It almost hurts how much I love the thing his lip does at the corner. "I'll come and get you at eight, okay?"

DAD COOKS HAMBURGERS on the barbecue like he does every Saturday. Lots tonight, because Betty and Frank have come up, and Frank's a big eater. Mom thinks he's a pig, in more ways than one, but she tolerates him because Betty has been her best friend since before they both got married.

I can hardly eat. While the rest of my family and my parents' friends are having watermelon, I look through my dresser for something to wear. With my white shorts, which show off my tan, I put on a green halter top that Gramma gave me. It has a nice soft t-shirty feel and ties behind my neck and behind my back. I turn my body to look at it from different angles in the mirror. It looks nice. I lean my face close to the mirror. In my grey eyes, I see tiny flecks of green and blue, and even a little gold.

"Not that thing, Nan. No." Mom is stretched out on a deck chair, her elbow resting on its arm. She waves her cigarette at me. "You can't even wear proper underwear with it." Before I can even take a breath to argue, she goes on, "The colour is nice on you, but your t-shirt from school would be much more suitable."

"You mean my *gym* shirt? You want me to wear my *gym* shirt to a dance?"

Betty chuckles. Probably at me, but maybe at Mom. She's the only person I know of who could get away with laughing at Mom. Come to think of it, the only times Mom ever laughs herself are when she's with Betty. Not all-out guffaws or anything, but enough so you can tell she's having a good time.

"You are not going out of here with that boy," Mom says, "wearing a shirt that's only half there. What kind of a girl do you want him to think you are?"

"I've worn it lots of times before and you never—"

"If you want to go to this dance, go and put on a proper shirt."

"Yeah, Ruby," Gary says. "Why don't you just do what Mom says for once?"

"Why don't you just shut your face, you miserable traitor?"

"Nan, that's no way to talk to your brother."

Tough titties, I'd like to say, but of course that would be *no way* to talk to my mother.

One by one I toss shirts out of my drawer onto the bed. Vile colour. Stains in the armpits. Too worn. My lovely gym shirt. Does she really think—? I will never understand how my mother thinks. I hold up my peasant blouse in front of me. It's white like my shorts, and has a bit of white embroidery on the front. How's this, Mom? Virginal enough for you? I pull it on over my head. Maybe not. If Daniel looks hard enough, he'll see my *proper underwear* right through it. But it does have a front and back. And it looks good with my tan.

The chastity guard is not exactly thrilled, but the shirt passes.

At eight o'clock, when my parents and their friends have moved inside to play cards, Daniel comes. He's still in his jean-shorts, but he's changed into a white t-shirt, and his bare feet are stuffed into running shoes. Gary glances up from his puzzle. Susie and April gawk as Daniel again assures Mom and Dad he'll have me home by eleven. I slip on my sandals and usher him out the door before anything can go wrong.

The air outside is fresh. We are on our way. We are going to the dance. *I* am going out *with Daniel.*

Half way up the driveway, he takes my hand. His feels warm and big around mine.

"You look nice," he says.

"You do too." Already the night is perfect.

CHAPTER
SIX

WHEN WE STEP INTO THE REC HALL, *Do You Wanna Dance* is playing on a record player set up in the corner. The room is dimly lit by candles on tables at the sides of the room and a few frosted pink bulbs hanging from the ceiling. Only a dozen or so couples are dancing.

"So, do you want to?" Daniel says. "Dance?"

"Okay." But the song ends, and there's nothing to do but stand there. A couple of guys come over.

"Hi, Chris. Marty." I recognize them as the guys Daniel was playing soccer with. The shorter of the two was also swimming at the park the night I first met Daniel. I wish they weren't here. Boys are always different with their friends around. "Remember Ruby?"

"Sure I remember," the short one says. "White bathing suit, right? You two want a lift anywhere later? I got wheels."

Behind my back my hands clench—I don't want to go anywhere with this guy.

Daniel says, "We'll get home on our own, thanks."

"I have got the picture, good buddy, and maybe I'll get lucky tonight too, and there'll be no room for you in my back seat anyway." Chris and Marty head across the room toward a couple of girls sitting at a table.

"Don't mind him," Daniel says, taking my hand.

The next record the disc jockey plays is a faster one. More people get up to dance, including Daniel's friends and the girls at the table. Daniel just sort of bounces on his feet and shakes his arms, and I more or less copy him. After that comes a slow song, and judging by how those girls are hanging on to Chris and Marty, I won't have to worry about them hanging around us tonight.

Daniel and I step toward each other, and our arms land around each other in the right places. My face leans hot against Daniel's chest.

"You smell good," I tell him.

"Jade East," he says.

It's not till after I agree that I realize what he said was just the name of his aftershave.

After a few more songs, we stop for a soft drink. Daniel's short of cash, and I didn't think to bring any, so we'll share. "Whatever you want to get," I say—it's his money.

Sitting at an empty table, I watch Daniel cross the room, admiring the slope of his shoulders and how easy his jean-shorts ride on his hips.

"I hope you like cream soda." He pulls the other chair around beside mine and puts the bottle on the table.

"Cream soda's good."

"I figured you'd like it."

"You did?"

"Yeah, it's kind of like you, isn't it?" Daniel holds the bottle over the candle in the middle of our table. Its flame lights up the drink inside. "Ruby-red and jewel-like?" He rolls his eyes like he knows he's being corny.

I feel like I'm watching myself in a movie. I can't believe that this conversation—this whole scene with this amazing guy—is really happening to me.

"You know what? I just got around to trying cream soda this summer, and after I did . . ."—it's incredible I want to tell him this—". . . is when I changed my name to Ruby." I don't tell him that hearing him say my name the way he does makes me determined to keep using it—always.

"Just like that, you changed your name?"

"Not exactly. It was already my first name, but I went by my middle name before."

"What's your middle name?"

"Darn, I should have known you'd ask me that."

"So what is it?"

I take a mouthful of our drink. Fruity sweetness fizzes against the roof of my mouth.

"If I tell you mine," Daniel says, "will you tell me yours?"

I swallow. "Okay."

"Egbert."

Egbert? He *voluntarily* told me his name is *Egbert?*

"Yup. After my great-grandfather." Daniel takes a drink. Some dribbles onto his chin. A big pink dribble of cream soda.

Anyone else in the world would want to crawl under the table and die of shame, but Daniel just wipes off his chin with the palm of his hand and says, "So what's your middle name?"

Nothing at all seems to embarrass this guy—he is a miracle—so telling him my middle name has become no big deal. "Nan. After the dog in *Peter Pan*," I claim.

"I think that was Nana."

"Oh yeah."

"Nan," Daniel says. He actually manages, somehow, to make it sound quite lovely. He could probably make even Gertrude and Mathilda, the names of Patty's hamsters, sound lovely.

"But my mom mostly calls me Nanny."

Daniel bleats like a goat.

"Exactly!" Together we bleat like a couple of idiot goats.

"You two having a good time?" one of Daniel's friends says, a girl on his arm as he passes our table.

"Yeah, Chris, we are," Daniel says, like there's nothing wrong with acting like farm animals at a dance.

After Chris is gone, Daniel says, "So why doesn't your Mom call you Ruby?"

I shrug. "I don't know. Maybe she wants me to be plain."

"You?"

He is saying he doesn't think I am. He's saying he thinks I'm better than plain. As I take another drink from the cream soda bottle, I'm aware that Daniel's lips have been where mine are now. Did he think of that when he took a drink after me? Can I taste Daniel's lips on the neck of the bottle, or is my imagination just doing a real good job tonight?

Will Daniel kiss me before it's over?

We leave the empty bottle on the table and our shoes underneath it and return to the dance floor. *Unchained Melody* vibrates through the wood floor boards up into our bare feet. I can feel the tips of Daniel's fingers, cool from our drink, through the back of my peasant blouse. And the heat of his palms.

The next song is a fast one by the Turtles. Waving his arms across from me, Daniel sings along. I can't hear his voice, but hear the words of *Happy Together* like I never have before. *I can't see me lovin' nobody but you, for all my life. When you're with me, baby, the skies'll be blue . . .*

Our bodies are hot after that one, but when *This Boy*

starts up, Daniel holds me close again, closer even than before. When I wrap my arms around his neck, my blouse rides up and his hands . . . oh . . . touch the skin of my back above the waistband of my shorts.

When the music speeds up, Daniel and I keep on dancing slow. *Good good good, good vibrations.* The hair on Daniel's thighs tickles mine. Through the next long slow dance, and the next, the sides of our feet touch too.

Then, time to get our shoes. Daniel's big runners and my sandals.

Walking back to the cottage, Daniel keeps his arm around me all the way, and we talk some more and look at the moon. It's ten to eleven when we get to the top of our drive-way. Daniel leads me into the grove of white pines. Before morning their needles will be heavy with dew. Right now their scent mixes with the Jade East of Daniel's neck. I'm not sure if the pulse I feel beating is his or my own.

His lips, when he kisses me, are full and soft. I kiss him back, my mouth open a little. I have never kissed a boy like that before. It's like the first early morning ripple on a smooth lake happening inside me.

"See you tomorrow," Daniel whispers, his lips still wet in the moonlight.

He walks me to the rectangle of yellow light into which I must go.

"Good night."

In the brightness of the cottage, Dad looks up from his newspaper. Betty and Frank have already gone to bed. "Did you have a nice time, Ruby?"

He can't see how I have changed since I left this room a few hours ago. I smile at him and nod.

Mom's surprise with herself that she let me go to the dance is showing now in the tightness around her mouth. "I hope that boy was *nice*?"

"Yes," I say, "he is." What she really wants to know, I'm sure, is that he didn't touch me once, not even when we were dancing. But Daniel did touch me, and I touched him, and we danced and kissed, and I want to do it all again and do it all some more.

My room is so warm I consider changing into my swimsuit and going in the lake before bed. But more than cooling off I want just to hold onto what Daniel has made me feel. I want to go on tasting where his lips have touched mine, go on smelling him on my hands and in my hair.

Without brushing my teeth and without turning on the light, I slip into my cool summer nightie. Lying in the dark I savour all the places our bodies have touched. And imagine Daniel touching magic places I am only myself beginning to find.

GARY SLIDES A BREAKFAST PLATE BACK into my dishpan of sudsy water. "Egg."

I swipe the cloth over it and again set it in the rack.

"Missed a spot." Gary splashes another plate back into the dishwater.

"Did not." When I pass it back, I let the edge catch the water and flip it across Gary's shirt.

He reaches into the dishpan and flicks suds in my face.

"You . . . !" I scoop up the sodden dishcloth as Gary bounces away from me into the living room, and Mom says, "Honestly, you two, can't you try to get along?"

"We're not serious," Gary tells her.

"Nan, get out of here with that thing. You're dripping all over the floor."

Back at the sink, Gary mutters, "Ha ha."

When he turns to put a glass in the cupboard, I give the cloth one last good squeeze down the back of his neck.

WHEN DANIEL COMES OVER, we sit outside on the back step. It turns out his parents only got the cottage for the weekend, and he's going home later that day. My heart sinks. But starting next week—and Dad's holidays will be over by then, so we'll be back home except for weekends— Daniel's going to be working at the Ex, not too far from where I live in the city. He'll be cleaning the Dominion booth in the Food Building and showing ladies to their seats in the kitchen theatre.

"Can you maybe come down and see me sometimes?"

"Yes."

And if I could turn myself into a broom, I would do that too, so Daniel could hold onto me the whole time he's working.

Watching Daniel saunter away, his thumbs hooked into his pockets, I'm dying to tell someone about how wonderful he is. Patty, of course, when we get home, but I'm going to tell Gramma about him too, the next time I see her, and about how good it feels to be with him. She won't act shocked, I know, or make like it's bad to feel what I do, or silly. Or pretend she doesn't know what I'm talking about, like Mom would if I ever tried talking to her about Daniel. As if. I bet Gramma might even tell me how she used to feel good being with Poppa too.

I hold my hands together between my knees and wonder how they feel to Daniel when he holds them.

CHAPTER
SEVEN

THE LAST DAYS AT THE COTTAGE DRAG by till finally we're loading up the station wagon for the trip back to the city. Patty comes over as soon as I call her.

She's dying to get a look at the guy who's got me so preoccupied I can't even pretend to be interested in helping her decide which eye shadow to wear, so she's happy to go to the Ex with me as soon as it opens. Which is good. Mom would never let me go down there on my own.

Crowds of people stream through the entrance to the fairgrounds and move like ants through the midway and the exhibit buildings. Daniel looks adorable in his grey knickers and yellow vest. All the other boys at the Dominion booth just look like goofs. I can tell Patty thinks Daniel looks goofy too, but she's a good enough friend not to say so. We can't talk long because Daniel's boss is pretty strict, but we arrange to meet as soon as he gets off work.

On the way out of the Food Building, Patty and I stop for free samples of french fries and a new brand of ice cream. We go on the roller coaster and the Rotor, eat waffles and more ice cream, and go see what's been sculpted out of butter this year. Then it's time to meet Daniel. Patty goes off to the Ferris wheel with a guy we met on the midway that afternoon, so I can meet Daniel by myself.

Between the concert pavilion and the lake, away from the crash of midway rides and rock music, lights sparkle off the black water. The breeze is cool. Daniel wraps me in his arms, and I tuck mine up inside the back of his jacket. Tonight he is Jade East and leather. We talk for a long time. It's easy with Daniel. Between sentences we kiss little kisses, like we just need to remind each other how we taste. As it gets closer to when I have to meet up with Patty to catch our bus home, our kisses grow longer.

I never knew before I could want a single kiss to be forever.

"YOU'RE LATE," Mom says when I get home.

"Sorry." I walk past her to my room. I'm not going to ruin a perfect evening arguing minutes on the clock with my mother.

THE NEXT DAY on his break, Daniel calls.

"What are you doing?"

I hold the phone to my ear with my shoulder. "Peeling potatoes for potato salad."

"You peel potatoes?"

"Yeah."

"And make potato salad?"

"It's not a big deal."

"If you're old enough to peel potatoes, you're old enough to get married."

I squeeze the phone hard against my ear. "Daniel, I'm not even sixteen till October."

"What do you think is the most important thing in life?"

"I dunno. I guess . . . to be happy."

"Me too." The weird thing is, as soon as I say that, *Happy Together,* which we danced to at the cottage, starts playing on the radio. Next to anything by the Beach Boys, it's our favourite song.

Every day on his break, Daniel phones me. We'd get together when he has a day off, but I can't talk Mom or Dad into letting me stay home from the cottage on the weekend. As the last bit of summer speeds by, it gets harder to ignore the awful fact that Daniel is staying at his aunt's only while the Ex is on. After Labour Day, he goes back home, to some town fifty miles away and so small it doesn't even have a bus passing through. Once school starts up, I'll probably never see Daniel again.

"PATTY AND ME are going to the Ex," I tell my mom. Even though the guy who went with Patty on the Ferris wheel turned out to be an eight-armed loser, and she realized she could never cheat on her regular boyfriend anyhow, I have managed to talk her into going down with me one more time.

"Patty and I," Mom corrects me as she swipes a sponge over the bathroom sink. "No, you're not."

"But it closes soon. We wanted to go one more time."

"Well maybe you should have thought of that when you didn't come home till close to midnight the last time you went."

"Come on, Mom. It was only twenty after eleven. It wasn't our fault we just barely missed a bus and had to wait half an hour for the next one."

In the doorway of the bathroom, Gary appears beside me. After his siding with Mom over the shirt I was going to wear to the dance, I want to warn him to buzz off, but don't dare risk Mom's using that as another reason to keep me home.

"Yeah, Mom," Gary says, "those buses are stupid. Half the time you get to a stop before one's even scheduled to come, and the bus has just left." And he continues, "It wouldn't have been Ruby's fault if she missed one."

Funny thing is, I don't think Gary's ever been *near* the buses downtown.

Mom rinses cleanser out of her sponge. "You stay out of this, Gary."

But isn't it nice, *Mom, that we're getting along?*

Gary shrugs and retreats to his room.

"I don't want you way down there again after dark." She puts down her sponge and lights a cigarette. "You don't know what kind of people might be riding the buses at night."

It is possible this is the real reason she doesn't want me at the Ex at night. It's also possible—because she's probably heard me on the phone—that she's figured out Daniel is working there, and has decided that letting me go to that dance was a big mistake that she's now got to correct. But she can't do this to me. It's almost noon. I've arranged to meet Daniel at two. Today is our last chance to see each other. Maybe forever. "What if I say we'll leave before it gets dark? Then can I go?" I do my best not to look desperate.

Trying—I can tell—to come up with a reason to say no, Mom holds onto a mouthful of smoke. I can taste it in my own mouth and want to spit.

"All right," she says like it hurts her, and exhales. "But I want you home for supper."

On my way out, I poke my head into Gary's room. "Thanks."

"Daniel seems okay."

"Yeah, he is. Sometimes you are too."

INSTEAD OF COMING ALL THE WAY to the Ex with me, Patty goes to see a matinee of *Barefoot in the Park*. Daniel and I meet outside the Food Building, near the start of the aerial car ride. We kiss briefly, and with his arm still around my shoulder he starts walking. I try to pull him to a stop so we can kiss some more—we've only got a couple of hours—but Daniel teases me about being a nymphomaniac and says there's something on the midway he wants me to see.

It's a big stuffed monkey. He blows three bucks trying to win it for me. When he reaches into his pocket for more quarters, I say, "Don't."

"I want you to have it."

"Why? It doesn't matter."

"I almost did it. I should have been able to—"

"Daniel, it's just a dumb monkey."

Right away I see I've hurt his feelings. But how can I say that what I meant was I don't want to waste precious time together watching him throw balls at a wall of holes?

On the roller coaster I'm so aware of time zooming by that I feel like I'm going to throw up.

Daniel gets me a drink of water after, and we sit on a bench. Not touching. Not talking. People all around us are eating waffles and ice cream, carrying oversized stuffed animals, fanning themselves with cardboard Shopsy's fans, yelling at their kids. I have to leave soon to go home.

Maybe we're both, Daniel and me, just trying to get used to being apart. Or maybe we were never really all that together; I just imagined it. Maybe Daniel should have just worked this afternoon. The sun blazes down on us and my head hurts. Someone walks by with a transistor radio. *I may not always love you, but long as there are stars above you* . . . The Beach Boys. *God only knows how much I lo-ove you* . . .

I didn't imagine anything.

Daniel says, "I can still call you."

"It won't be the same though, will it, when it's long distance."

"No." Daniel's leg jiggles up and down like he hates this conversation as much as I do. "It probably won't be able to be very often." He places his hands on his thighs to still them. "Or for very long."

I fiddle with a loose thread in the seam of my jeans. "Daniel, remember that morning in the park after the night we swam?"

"Yeah, sort of."

"Do you remember what you said to me?"

"Not really."

"Don't you?"

I stare into Daniel's brown eyes. *You can touch it if you want.* I think it over and over. I know he said it. *You can touch it if you want.*

"Yes," he says. "I do remember."

"Can I?"

"Now? Here?" People are jostling by all around us. The sun is almost dazzling.

"Yeah."

Daniel looks at me, his eyes softening. He untucks his t-shirt from his jeans and pulls it off over his head. He balls it up in his lap and sits perfectly still. The man at a nearby caravan guesses the age of a woman who shrieks when he gets it right.

For a long moment, I just look at the scar, the white crescent moon of flesh in the dark skin of Daniel's shoulder. It is as perfect as I remember.

Watching Daniel's face, I place my finger at one end of his scar. He closes his eyes. I can feel him holding his breath. Through the tip of my finger slowly tracing the curve, his skin is hot. If we were alone, I would put my lips to Daniel's scar. With my tongue I would see how it tastes.

"Ruby," Daniel whispers, "I think you better stop."

CHAPTER
EIGHT

ORDINARILY I LIKE SEPTEMBER—getting back to school, seeing people again, finding out who my teachers are. Packages of blank looseleaf paper and new textbooks always give me that fresh-new-beginning feeling I first had with my sharp new pencil and clean eraser in grade one. But this year I don't want a fresh new start. I want Daniel. If only he didn't live so far away, or if phoning long distance didn't cost so darn much.

After lunch one day Mom brings a bag out of her bedroom. "I've bought you and Susie new blouses for back-to-school." April won't start school till next year.

Susie's blouse has red and white stripes, up and down, and a crisp red tie in the front. Its middy collar hangs smartly across her shoulders. Susie puts it on and models it for Dad, sitting at the kitchen table eating an extra cheese sandwich before going out to fix more plumbing.

"See, Daddy? I can wear the sleeves like this . . ." She flips up the edge to make a cuff. "Or like this!"

My blouse is pale, almost-blue. Not blue enough to have a name, like 'cornflower,' and certainly not 'royal' or 'navy' or 'indigo.' It looks like a blouse that started out white but got mixed with blue towels in the wash. It doesn't have a tie or a collar. It doesn't even have sleeves.

"Mom?"

She sucks on her cigarette.

"Did that blouse . . ." I nod, casually, toward Susie. "Did it come in other sizes?"

A stream of cigarette smoke shoots from Mom's lips. She laughs and to Dad says, "I told you Nanny'd be jealous, didn't I?"

I hurry from the kitchen, blinking back tears. I can't believe I'm crying over a stupid blouse. So Susie got a nicer one than me. Big deal. It's not the first time. But she *knew*. Mom *knew* she was doing it. She probably knows what she's doing when she calls me Nanny too. As if *Nan* isn't bad enough. Does it matter to her so much that I never get what I want?

It's not just what Patty says—that mothers have a hard time seeing daughters grow up, especially after puberty. Mine has been like this since I was little. I heard her once telling a neighbour, whose kid was starting school, "When Nanny started kindergarten she cried at school every day—

every day!—and the teacher eventually called me in to talk about it. 'Nanny loves school,' I told her." Mom repeated the whole conversation like it was this big thing she was proud of.

"She asked me, 'Is there anything happening at home that might be making Nan so unhappy?'

"I said to her, 'Not at all. Tell me—what do you do when Nanny cries?'

"'I let her sit on my lap,' the teacher said, 'and after a few minutes, she's happy to go off to play with the other children.'

"'Let me suggest,'" Mom said she said, and I can hear her saying it too—*Let me suggest*—as if a person has any choice in the matter, "'that when Nanny cries, you *don't* put her on your lap. I am sure she is just looking for attention.'

"And you know," Mom said to the neighbour, "I was right. A few days after the teacher stopped letting Nan up on her lap—no more tears."

I like to think the neighbour told my mother what a heartless skunk she was, but I didn't hear what she said.

Stupid how I still remember that. Stupid how much it still hurts that Mom basically told that teacher, 'Don't be nice to my daughter.'

Susie, now in her play-clothes, passes by the living room. Before heading outside she looks at me with a mix, I think, of smugness and pity.

I'd like to go into Susie's room and take Mom's lighter with me. I'd like to flip open its top, smell the oily fluid inside, flick the ignitor, and put the flame to those red and white stripes, to that middy collar and tie.

But instead I just go hang my new blouse, ready for the start of grade eleven, in my closet.

MY NEW HOME ROOM TEACHER is Mrs. Moffatt. She's a mix of sergeant major and Earth Mother, the kind of teacher I want to be when I grow up, only for younger kids. Strict, but not too strict, and all the kids will come to me with their problems.

I wonder what Daniel wants to be when he finishes school.

In guidance class toward the end of the second week of school—and it looks like Daniel was right, he's not going to be able to call me much, and I miss him so much already—Mrs. Moffatt lines the chalk ledge with stacks of information sheets about different jobs. She invites us up to take copies of whatever we want. "Please keep your minds open to the many opportunities."

I collect chalk dust on my finger as I walk along the display of pamphlets. I'm keeping my eye out for *You Can Be A Teacher!* But before I find it, I notice the concerned expression on a woman's face on one of the other sheets. It reminds me of Mrs. Moffatt the day she helped me get excused from gym when my cramps were really bad. *You Can Be A Social Worker!* it says. I tuck the social worker pamphlet into the front of my binder, where I'll remember to take it home. Before I find the teacher pamphlet, the bell goes, telling us to move on to our next class.

Alone in my room after school, I sprawl on my nubby bedspread and read about family problems like alcoholism, unemployment, gambling, poverty. I never knew anything about social workers before, how they get involved to help people.

Mom calls down the hall. It's time for me to peel the potatoes.

The worst part about peeling potatoes is reaching into the dark bag to get them. Their eyes feel so gross when you can't see what you're touching. And you never know when there'll be a potato that's soft and rotting, and it'll mush all smelly in your hand when you grab hold of it. After that happened to me once, I brought the bag out of the cupboard and tried dumping the potatoes I'd need into the sink so I wouldn't have to touch any till I could see them. But Mom chewed me out about getting too much dirt in the sink that way. When I told her why I was doing it, she said, "Don't be ridiculous," as if she herself didn't mind getting her hand covered in potato slime.

All seven of today's potatoes, one for each of us except two for my dad, are firm and dry. I stand at the sink and see

how many of them I can peel in one long strip. I remember
Daniel's amazement that I was peeling potatoes once when
he called. I wish he would call now. I know he warned me
he'd probably hardly ever be able to because of long distance
being too expensive for having real conversations, but still,
just to hear his voice again . . . I should have asked him for
his number.

I'm almost done when Mom comes up from the basement and heads down the hall, the laundry basket piled high
with clean clothes. When she comes back to the kitchen, I
just have to rinse the potatoes and cut them into quarters.

"What's this?" Mom asks. She's holding out *You Can Be A
Social Worker!* like it's *True Confessions* magazine or something equally, in her opinion, scandalous.

"Mrs. Moffatt brought in these pamphlets today about
different jobs."

"This isn't about teaching."

"I know. I'm thinking about maybe being a social worker
instead."

"But you've always wanted to be a teacher. And really, Nan
. . . believe me, there are *some* people you simply *do not* want
to work with."

Why, again, do I feel so . . . dismissed? It's as if nothing I
ever want, or think even, has any validity.

Gary says to me later, when we're doing dishes and Mom
and Dad are out at Couples' Club at the church, "I heard

what Mom said to you. She doesn't want me to be a carpenter either."

"You're kidding. Why not?"

"Who knows? Slivers?"

I look at my brother like I haven't in a long time. That he might sometimes find Mom as difficult as I do has never occurred to me before. But of course, now that I think of it, there is that look she always gives him whenever he says he's going over to Wayne's.

"Does it seem like she never wants anyone to have what they want?"

Gary shrugs. "I figure there's probably something she wanted once and couldn't have, so now she takes out her disappointment on everybody else."

Again Gary has surprised me. For such a dumb guy, he just might turn out to be half smart.

WHEN I COME IN FROM PATTY's one day, Mom and Susie are sitting together on the couch, a catalogue open on Mom's lap. Mom's saying to Susie, "Aren't these dresses with the smocking across the chest beautiful?"

"They're pretty," Susie agrees. She looks up and says, "New sale catalogue came today. Want to look at it with us?"

"No thanks."

It used to be one of my favourite things. Curling my feet underneath me like Mom did and poring over the pages, mixing and matching blouses and skirts, pants and sweaters, a few of which I might actually get to have. Mom always seemed relaxed looking at the catalogue, and I remember her softly stroking my hand sometimes as we chatted about clothes or how the models wore their hair. I liked how her long fingernails felt, soft against my skin. I sometimes wished she'd uncurl her fingers a bit so I could feel their tips instead of her nails. When she moved her hand away to point out a certain dress or to light a cigarette, I just wished she would touch me again.

Lately looking at the catalogue together has become some kind of test I usually fail. I point out a dress I like and Mom will say, "That zipper up the front isn't very attractive though, is it?" Of course the zipper was exactly what I liked. Or Mom will point to a navy pleated skirt and white blouse, "Now, this looks smart." Maybe that was the last time we did the catalogue thing, when instead of agreeing whole-heartedly—because I didn't want to end up with a navy skirt and white blouse for my birthday—I said, diplomatically I thought, "For a singer in St. Bart's choir." Mom sighed her sigh that says I have no idea at all about how to dress nicely and why do I have to be such a hopelessly disagreeable cuss anyway?

As I hang my jacket in the closet, Mom says to Susie, "I can't imagine who would want to wear those colours together. Can you?"

"No," Susie says, "I can't."

Later Susie comes to my room. She whispers, "Hey, Ruby, those colours Mom hated?"

I look up from my homework.

"They were *fabulous*. Green and this amazing shade of purple. Do you think maybe Gramma would buy me the outfit?"

IN THE SWIMSUIT Gramma bought me in the summer, I shiver at the side of the pool. Why do girls and boys have to take swimming together, I wonder, when all our other gym classes are separate? Why did I like it when Daniel looked at me almost naked, but when any of the boys at school do, I just feel lumpish?

"Nice suit, Nan," one of them says. "Those flames look really hot."

"Ha ha, good one, Larry. And I'm going by Ruby now, remember?"

Larry blushes. "Oh, yeah." He wasn't making a joke, I realize, and I've just put down his compliment. Before I can figure out if I can fix it, the teacher orders the boys into the pool, and Larry's the first one in.

Later, as our class piles out of the science room, I hear Larry say, "Ask Ruby."

"Ruby?" Keith says.

"Yeah, she used to be Nan."

"Yeah, I know, but . . ."

I wrap my arms around my books and feel my shoulders creeping up around my ears. I've had a crush on Keith since grade seven, but I don't think we've ever said a word to each other. He's no Daniel, but still—

Larry whispers something I don't hear, then says, "Just ask her."

I muster my courage to turn and say, as casually as I can, "Ask me what?"

Keith says, "Just something in today's Science." He moves close enough beside me that our sleeves touch. "I understand about how different animals fit into different groups, like birds and reptiles and stuff, according to their characteristics, right?"

"I hope so, Keith. That's pretty basic." Did that sound flirty? I hope it didn't sound know-it-all.

Keith looks at me like he really needs my help.

"Sorry. What is it you don't get?"

"Well, reptiles and amphibians lay eggs, and mammals bear their young, right?"

"Right."

"And people are mammals."

"Yes."

Keith glances toward Larry and goes on. "And only mammals have mammary glands, right?"

"Right."

"So . . . what are they?"

"What are what?"

"Mammary glands."

This seems pretty basic too, but Keith looks so genuinely embarrassed that I answer him as simply as I can. "They're how mothers feed their young."

Keith is still looking blank.

"You know . . . milk. The mammary glands produce milk and deliver it to the young through the mother's nipples."

The hall feels suddenly full of people. It's as if not one of them has been having a conversation, and all of them are looking at me. I may as well have shouted down the length of the hall, "Hey, everybody, look at my nipples!" Heat creeps up my neck and face like ink in a blotter.

Loudly now, Keith says, "Ruby, will you come over to my house after school and help me with my mammary glands homework?"

A set-up. The whole stupid thing. Every person in the hall is, of course, laughing. It's like a scene in one of those warning-against-drugs movies where the faces and sounds around me are all distorted, too big. My head pounds with humiliation.

Another guy says, "I don't know how much help Ruby can be. I'd ask Norma to come over if I were you. Now *there's* a girl who knows mammary glands."

Like an emergency exit that appears in a cartoon the moment some loser character is about to be eaten alive, the door to the girls' washroom appears beside me. I hurl myself through it and lock myself into a cubicle.

Idiot, idiot, idiot! I should have been able to see what was coming. If I was more like . . . Wendy say, I could even have fallen for the *I don't understand* act but still not come out of it looking so stupid. She probably would have played right along with the idea of going to Keith's, and even the crack about Norma wouldn't have fazed her. She probably would have said something clever, like *Norma may know more than I do, my dear Keith, but I would be happy to share with you all I do know.* She'd have made herself sound so sexy saying it, everyone would have been laughing at Keith in the end instead of at her. She certainly wouldn't be hiding out in some stupid washroom and waiting for the racket of changing classes out in the hall to end.

Gradually the hall noise dies. History class will have already begun. There's no way I'm walking in late and giving everyone the chance to look up and snicker. I head to my locker, dump in my books and go home.

Mom is on her knees in the bathroom, full of the smell of cleanser. "You're early." She sloshes a wet rag around the rim of the toilet and flushes.

"Cramps," I tell her and keep walking to my room.

Now that I'm home I wonder why I didn't go to the mall or something till it was the normal time to come home, but it's too late for that now. It doesn't matter. I can make some more headway with that book I've been reading, about a schoolteacher up in some little mountain community. Mom recommended it, and I know what she's trying to do—*See how satisfying being a schoolteacher can be?* How subtle. But the book is actually pretty good. Most of the people up that mountain could do with a good social worker too. In a way that's what this teacher is.

After a while Susie comes home just long enough to say she's going to her friend Debbie's. I keep on reading. One of the older students is coming on to the teacher, who's hardly older than he is. I look up to see why Mom is standing in the doorway.

"Gramma!" I set my book face down on my night stand. "I didn't know you were coming today!"

"We had to cancel bridge tonight 'cause one of the girls is having her gall bladder out."

It's funny how Gramma calls the old ladies she plays cards with *girls*.

"I thought I might as well come have dinner with my favourite grandchildren."

Gramma's careful to include the others, and she does love them too of course, but I know it's really me she has a special feeling for. Gramma lies down on the bed beside me.

"Your mother tells me you've got cramps."

Rather than tell her I lied, which I don't know if Gramma
would approve of even if I am her favourite granddaughter,
I say, "They're not bothering me now."

"I'm surprised you'd come home with them, Ruby. You
usually just carry on like a trouper through all that nonsense."

So she knows I never did have cramps today. But she
doesn't say anything more about it, just waits to see if I want
to tell her why I really came home early.

"Damage control," I say.

"What kind of damage?"

"I let this guy at school trick me into telling him something really embarrassing that, of course, he already knew.
Sometimes I can be so dumb."

"Coming home probably wasn't such a dumb thing. By
tomorrow everyone will have forgotten all about it."
Gramma, with her hands behind her head, seems to be
studying the pattern of cracks in my ceiling. She looks a little
pale, the effect of the late afternoon light probably. "But you
don't think you could have told your mom what you told
me, instead of making up some excuse about cramps?"

"I don't know. She would have thought I was being silly.
She probably would have made me go back to school or
something."

Gramma chuckles. "Your poppa was like that, you know.
Judging other people harshly. But not any more harshly
than he judged himself. And your mother does want the

best for you kids, just like Poppa did for her. You know that, don't you?"

From down the hall Mom calls, "You two slackers going to lie around till supper's ready? How about coming and giving me a hand?"

I grate carrots, Gramma chops cabbage, and Mom mixes up the muck for salmon loaf. By the time we're finished, everybody else is home and the house is too full for any more private little chats. I realize I never even started telling Gramma about Daniel.

We eat in the dining room whenever we have company. Soon after we sit down, Susie's in the middle of telling Gramma about some game she played with Debbie, when Mom says, "Ted?" She gives him a look and he takes his elbows down off the table.

On the wall behind Dad is a portrait of my parents on their wedding day. I've seen it often, but tonight, chewing a mouthful of cabbage buried in potato in hopes of disguising the taste, I wonder what they saw in each other then. They were both really good-looking—Dad still is—but there must have been more than that to their deciding they wanted to spend the rest of their lives together.

After supper I ask Gramma, "Can you stay over?"

"No, darlin'. I have a doctor's appointment early in the morning, before work, and with the extra bus, it takes too long to get downtown from here. But I'll be back soon."

Maybe I'll tell Gramma about Daniel then, and get her to talk to me more about what my parents were like when they were young, and how it is she thinks that Mom wants the best for me.

CHAPTER
NINE

IMAGINE ME AND YOU, I do—

I crank up the music on my radio. Who cares about homework anyway, when the whole weekend lies ahead? *I think about you day and night, it's only ri-i-ight.* Laying my head on my math book, I let the song infuse me with the feelings of summer. *So happy to-ge-e-ther* . . . The phone rings. I turn down the volume in case it's Patty.

Mom calls from the kitchen, "For you, Nan."

"Hello."

"Can I come see you? I want to see you."

"Yes!" I shiver cold and hot at the same time. "But how—?"

"My thumb. So I can't say what time exactly, but after supper. Is that okay?"

Okay? That Daniel is coming at all is perfect.

"I'll see you as soon as I can."

The phone buzzes in my ear. Back in my room, the radio's only playing an ad for pimple cream, but I crank the volume back up anyway.

I don't say anything all through supper, but clearing away the plates, I tell Mom, "Remember Daniel, from the cottage? He's coming over tonight."

Mom blows smoke out the corner of her mouth. "That's nice."

"We'll probably go over to the Friday Night Drop-in at the church."

She never objects to anything if it's happening at the church.

Dishes done, it's starting to get dark. Betty and Frank show up to play Canasta with my parents. Betty brings four pastries with her and makes some lewd comment about them that I don't quite catch, but Mom chortles as she sets them out on a plate. Frank starts telling a farmer's daughter joke.

Daniel still hasn't come. To get away from the sound of people having a good time, I go to my room and try to finish my math. But it doesn't stop me worrying. Did Daniel get lost? Did the wrong kind of person stop to give him a ride? Did his mom stop him from coming? But he would have called then, wouldn't he? Unless he wasn't allowed to make another long distance call.

Gary, passing my room, says, "He'll come."

With my sweater on, ready to go out the instant Daniel arrives, I wander out to the kitchen, glance toward the front door, get a cookie from the cupboard. Mom comes in from the dining room. The only thing that could make it worse than if Daniel didn't come after all would be the sanctimonious look on Mom's face. When the telephone rings, I beat her to it. "Hello?"

"Hi, Babe. You going to Coffee House tonight?" Patty.

Mom pokes the last bite of her pastry into my mouth.

"Later maybe," I say, my mouth full. "Daniel's . . ." Mom's gone back to the card game, but I won't say *supposed to be* in case she can still hear. ". . . coming over."

"You all right? You sound funny."

"I'm fine." I can't say I thought Daniel would be here by now.

Through the frosted glass of the front door, I see someone coming up the front porch. "Patty, I gotta go."

I slam down the phone, make sure I don't have pastry stuck to my face, race across the kitchen, then slowly and nonchalantly walk through the hallway and vestibule.

When I step outside to meet him, Daniel says, "Sorry I'm late. It took a while to get picked up."

"Oh, are you late?" I ask, the way Patty would say I should, but I'm sure I don't fool either of us.

For a second we just look at each other, as if, in the weeks we've been apart, we have forgotten how to be together.

Then at the same moment we move toward each other. My arms slide up inside Daniel's jacket, and it feels so right to be wrapped up again in his arms and Jade East.

"I'm glad you're here."

"Me too," he says. "I think about you all the time. Tonight I just had to come."

I call inside, "We're going to Coffee House, 'kay?" To Daniel I mutter, "It's a Friday night drop-in thing at the church."

Daniel's arm fits perfectly around my shoulders as we wander up the street. We could just walk together all night and not go anywhere. But it'll be fun to see the looks on my friends' faces when I walk in with this gorgeous guy. Patty is the only one who has met him.

Before we pull open the heavy wooden door of the church and go inside, Daniel kisses me. Like always, kissing Daniel makes me feel like kissing him more.

Downstairs, music is playing. Something by the Beatles. People are sitting at most of the tables set up around the room—playing euchre, chatting, or just listening to the music. Someone is burning incense.

As Daniel and I approach their table, Patty, her boyfriend, Ray, and two of our other friends set down their cards. I try not to squeeze Daniel's hand too tightly as I look up at that lip of his that curls at one corner. Daniel smiles as I introduce him. His smile shows the chipped tooth that is so sexy, and I pull him away to an empty table in the corner.

While all around us people go on with their euchre games and conversations just like it was any other Friday, Daniel's long-fingered hands hold mine. We catch up on what's been happening since we last saw each other, which is nothing much. The speakers blare *Good good good—good vibrations*. I watch Daniel's lips as he kisses my fingers. He leans across the table to really kiss me, and when I can no longer stand being in the room with other people, we slip away to the quiet of the church.

The streetlights shining through the stained glass windows throw splotches of colour on some of the pews. I lead Daniel by the hand to a dark corner and we sit down.

"You know your scar?"

"Yeah."

"How did you get it?"

"Chain saw. I was working with my uncle on some stuff. It slipped."

"You could have died."

Daniel shrugs. "I guess."

Kissing Daniel in the church, snuggled under his arm in the pew, feels deliciously naughty. I slip my hand up the sleeve of his t-shirt to touch his scar. *Vibrations keep happening*. I want us to be still closer. I move onto his lap.

Daniel's face registers his surprise. He whispers, "And what would you like for Christmas, little girl?"

"I don't think I can tell you that in a church." We kiss some more and I wouldn't mind at all if Daniel wanted to touch my breasts. But he doesn't try to, and I'm not brave enough to slide his hand up from my waist myself.

After a while, before Reverend Tom makes his rounds and catches us where we shouldn't be, we go back to the drop-in. We take over a euchre game from Patty and Ray's opponents, who are heading out, and we are one hot euchre team. Daniel and Ruby. Ruby and Daniel.

At midnight, when Reverend Tom shows up to lock the doors, we step into the cool quiet of sleeping streets.

"Will it be hard to get a ride back this late?"

"Probably, but that's okay."

"I wish you didn't have to go." "I wish we had more time." Our words tumble together. We laugh, but it's sad. Not like in the summer, when our laughter was like the sweet fizz in a bottle of cream soda.

Between streetlights we stop walking and again we taste each other's lips.

"Ruby—" I love how my name sounds when Daniel says it. I love discovering new things about his face, like the laugh line beside one of his eyes even when he's being serious, the tiny mole at his jaw line. "Would it be okay if I stayed over at your place tonight? On the couch or something?"

"I . . ." Mom would never let that happen. "Your parents won't mind if you don't come home?"

"With my two older brothers, they've got used to a lot worse." Daniel looks down into my face and touches the skin beside my mouth. "Tonight wasn't enough time. I want to see you some more tomorrow before I have to head back home."

I want that too, of course. And I can't not even ask if Daniel can stay over. It's not like I'd be suggesting he could sleep in my bed or something. "I'll ask my mom." A breeze flutters the leaves on a tree. One falls.

We start walking again, cross the road, and at the curb I trip. I grab Daniel's waist to keep from falling. Wrapped around each other, not caring about the bright light above us, we kiss again, long moist kisses that feel like forever.

"ABSOLUTELY NOT," Mom says. "We know nothing about this boy. He didn't even come inside when he got here."

"You were busy with Betty and Frank." I shouldn't have told Daniel to wait on the porch. I was afraid of what Mom might say, but he can probably hear her anyway, and he did manage to talk Mom into letting me go to the dance that time. "Besides, you met Daniel at the cottage. I think you even sort of liked him."

"I know where I met him. But tell me, Nan, what kind of family does this boy come from that they let their son hitch-hike all over the countryside then expect a bed wherever he ends up?"

"My name is Ruby, *this boy's* name is Daniel, and he didn't exactly *end up* here. He came to see me, because he likes me. And he didn't expect a bed. The couch would be fine, he said."

She can't send him home tonight, she just can't, but the set of her eyebrow says she is not softening on this.

"If you don't want him in the house, we could lend him a sleeping bag," I suggest, "and he could sleep on the picnic table in the backyard."

"Oh, yes, that would be ever so much more respectable." Mom stubs her cigarette in the heaping ashtray beside her.

"So, what do you want him to do? Hitch all the way back home tonight?"

"No. Your father will drive him."

"Mo-om!"

"I said—your father will drive him home. We discussed what to do while you were out."

Mom looks at Dad. He gets up from his chair, takes his keys from his pants pocket, and walks out of the room.

I want to pick up my mother's ashtray and hurl it. Send it smashing against the wall. Butts and ashes everywhere, leaving a filthy trail.

Outside, I lean into Daniel's chest. "I'm sorry. I don't know what—" Our station wagon rolls out of the garage and stops beside the porch.

Daniel eases me away, hurries down the steps and opens the passenger door. "It's okay, Mr. Larkin. You don't have to do this. Really, I'll just—"

"I don't mind," Dad says. "I don't mind at all. Ruby's mother wouldn't sleep a wink if she knew you were hitchhiking."

I shake my head but cannot trust myself to speak. She couldn't care less what happens to Daniel, and the round trip to where Daniel lives and back will take hours.

Daniel climbs into the back seat. I slide in beside him, my denim thigh pressed against his.

"This is awful nice of you, Mr. Larkin. But I don't mind hitching back, you know—really."

"It's okay."

From the porch my mother is calling something. I roll down my window. "What did you say?"

"You heard me. You're staying here."

I reach in the dark for Daniel's hand, twine my fingers in his. "Why can't I go?"

"At this hour, you're going nowhere but bed. Your father can get the young man home perfectly well without your help."

Dad stares straight ahead.

"But—"

Daniel mumbles, "Don't, Ruby. You'll just make it worse." He lets go of my hand. His lips kiss the air between us. In the light over the porch, smoke drifts up my mother's face. She stares into the back seat of the car, waiting.

In a flash of daring, I lean over to Daniel and taste the softness of his cheek for the shortest of seconds and breathe in Jade East and the leather of his jacket. I want his lips, his skin, all of him. But he's right, I don't want to make things worse. Especially not for him. I whisper, "I'm really sorry, Daniel," and force myself to open the car door and climb out.

As I stomp up the steps of the porch, Mom grabs my wrist and says, as if she thinks she's a normal reasonable person, "Nan, you do understand, we can't just go opening our house up to strangers."

When I yank my arm away, her fingernail rips the skin.

CHAPTER
TEN

THE SKY IS OVERCAST, and it's cool enough outside to need a jacket. Most of the trees in the park across from my house have started losing their leaves. The climber and the swings, the sandbox and the slide are empty of children. I haven't heard from Daniel since he was here. It's been almost two weeks. It could just be the usual reason, or it could be that he's never going to call me again. I wrap my hands in my sleeves, park myself on a swing, and let it sway me gently back and forth on its long chains.

Gary thinks Daniel will call again, but what if Dad said something awful to him in the car that night? Or what if Mom's insistence he be driven home was so mortifying he's not ever going to come again? Is there something *I* said, or did? Maybe I shouldn't have kissed him in the car, with Dad there. Even if it was just on the cheek.

I can't stand being out here, where I won't hear the phone if it rings, but can't stand being in the house, where it's not ringing. I hop off the swing and walk over to Patty's, just down the street.

"Patty, if I pay you for it, can I try calling Daniel on your phone? I can't stand that he hasn't called, so I called information to get his number, but even if I could ever use the phone at home without somebody being around to hear, Daniel's would be the only long distance number to show up on our bill. My parents know where he lives, they'd know—"

"It's okay, Babe," Patty says. "You don't have to explain."

We go down to her rec room, where there's an extra phone. I hold the slip of paper with Daniel's number written on it and lift the receiver.

I slam it back down. "Oh, Patty, what if he's not home? What if he doesn't want to talk to me?"

"Of course he wants to talk to you. I saw how he looked at you at Coffee House that night. Just call him."

I press the receiver to my ear as Daniel's phone rings. Seven times it rings.

"Yeah?" A gruff voice. I'm not sure if it's a man's or a woman's.

"Um . . . is Daniel there, please?"

"Eh? Speak up."

I clear my throat. "I said, is Daniel there, please?" Maybe they just call him Dan at home, or Danny.

"I dunno, I doubt it."

"Could you check for me? Would you mind?"

"Naw, he ain't here."

I know she didn't check. "Well then, could you please tell him that Ruby called?"

"Yeah, yeah, Rudy, sure."

Before I can tell her it's *Ruby,* a dial tone is buzzing in my ear.

"Brother," I say to Patty. "I don't know if she was deaf or drunk or what."

"Daniel's mom?"

"I guess so. I don't know. I wonder if it could have been the wrong number."

WHEN I GET HOME FROM SCHOOL the next day, Mom's armchair in the corner of the living room is empty. Instead of one of Mom's soap operas, I hear Dad's voice. He should be at work, but I can see him from the vestibule. He's standing by the fridge, while Mom sits stiffly at the end of the kitchen table.

Every surface, the very air around me, has somehow become delicate. Gently I lay my math and history books on the counter. "What's wrong?"

When Mom reaches for a cigarette from the open package on the table, her hands are shaking. Something must be very wrong.

Outside the kitchen window, a single sparrow lands on a tree branch.

"Your grandmother . . ." Dad says. "You know the doctor sent her for some tests."

"No. I didn't know."

"Well . . . he did."

"Nobody told me. What kind of tests?"

"She'd found a lump."

Inside a cloud of smoke, Mom has not yet spoken.

"And?"

Dad says, "Your grandmother has cancer, Ruby."

Prickles skitter down between my breasts.

" . . . there are treatments, but . . ."

I can't breathe, can barely speak. "But . . . ?"

Dad shakes his head, so slightly it's as if he too feels the air of the room must not be disturbed. I turn to my mother, but she will not lift her eyes from the table.

"It's pretty extensive, Ruby," Dad says. "I . . ."

Inside me everything is cracking. I want to melt against Dad's chest. But the last time he hugged me was three years ago, when Poppa died.

"Can I see her? When can I see her?"

Mom speaks. "Not now." She looks, somehow, as if she is five years old, even as she slowly sucks on her cigarette and barely removes it from between her lips.

"Then when, Mom? I have to see her."

She lets the smoke drift up her face in thick swirls. The sparrow outside takes off from its branch.

Is Gramma going to die?

She can't.

CHAPTER
ELEVEN

PATTY SETS DOWN HER CAFETERIA TRAY and sits across from me. "Was that Blake Fuller? Here? Talking to you?"

"Yeah."

"What did he want?"

"Nothing important."

"Don't try to be cute, Ruby. Everybody knows he and Wendy have broken up. What did he want?"

"He asked me to the Hallowe'en dance, but put your eyeballs back in your head, okay. I'm not going."

"Do you know how many girls would give their right you-know-what to go out with Blake Fuller?"

"Guess I'm not like those other girls."

"Listen. Is this still about Daniel?"

It might be about Daniel, or it might be that with Gramma sick, I just can't get worked up about anything else, not even the cutest, most popular guy in the school. I shrug, and take a bite of my cheese sandwich. I haven't told Patty about my grandmother yet. I don't want to make it that serious, that real.

"Come on, Babe. Daniel was cute, but mooning around after a guy you're probably never going to hear from again— don't look at me like that, you said so yourself—isn't good. Here, want some of my fries?"

"Thanks." I dip a french fry in Patty's ketchup.

"Besides," Patty's campaign continues, "the Hallowe'en dance is always the best. Why *not* go with Blake? Imagine that car of his pulling up in your driveway."

"It's just a car, Patty."

"But it's his own. And it's a convertible."

"I don't think that's likely to be a big plus at the end of October."

"But you'll go. Won't you? Oh, Ruby, say yes."

I take another fry from Patty's plate, dip it in the ketchup and nibble it slowly. In a way I wouldn't mind showing up at the dance with one of the most popular guys in the school. It would sure make Larry and Keith look twice, if that's worth anything.

"Who knows?" Patty says. "Maybe Daniel will pick up the vibes of you being with another guy and smarten up and call you."

"Yeah, I wish."

"Haven't you ever noticed how either no one is interested in you or else a whole bunch of guys are?"

"No, Patty, I haven't."

"Well, it's like that a lot. It's got to do with territorial rights in apes or something. When Daniel senses there's someone else sniffing around his territory, he'll go ape."

Patty's theories of human behaviour—what can I do but laugh?

I dip one more fry in Patty's ketchup. "Okay, I'll go." Not because of Ape Theory, but because she's right. What do I have to lose? And how does that old song go? *Only lo-ove can break a heart. Only lo-ove can me-e-end i-it again.*

"With Blake? To the dance?"

"No. With Tarzan to the Lost Lagoon. Yes, with Blake, to the dance."

"Great, Ruby. That's great. Are you going to go tell him now? Do you want me to tell him?"

Blake is at a table on the other side of the cafeteria with three other guys from the basketball team. "Don't you dare. I'll tell him. Later."

IT'S NOT THAT EASY to catch Blake by himself, but when he leaves Biology class early, I excuse myself to go to the washroom.

I catch up with Blake at his locker. He looks down at me and smiles. "Ruby."

"Hi." He's taller than I remember. "You know how you . . . well, remember you . . ."

"Asked you to the dance?"

"Yeah, to the dance. Well, I'll go—if you still want. If you haven't asked someone else."

"No. I asked you."

"Yeah, well, I'll go."

"Great. So, can I pick you up at eight thirty?"

It's still a couple of weeks away, but I tell him where I live. "My parents are pretty strict," I add. "I'll probably have to be home by eleven thirty."

"That's all right. Would it be better if I parked around the corner? Some of the girls I've been out with—their parents get a bit tense when they see the car."

In a way I wouldn't mind parking Blake's car in Mom's face. *You thought Daniel was bad? Try this one.* But—"Yeah, okay. That's probably a good idea."

MOM IS WATCHING *The Secret Storm* when I get home from school. In my room I start my homework. When the Beach Boys come on the radio, I crank it up.

Mom calls down the hall, "Your father's home, Nan. Let's go." She sounds tired. "We have to go buy winter boots for you and April. Now. Before April gets hungry and the stores run out of your sizes."

In October? I sigh and turn off the radio—*Surfer Girl* is finished anyway. Arranging my mouth in the mirror, I press the creamy Coral Pearl I borrowed from Patty along my lips.

"Nan, must you wear those awful running shoes?" Mom stuffs her cigarettes and lighter into her purse. At the door, Dad waits patiently, the family chauffeur.

"I like these shoes. And *must* you call me Nan?"

"Go put on your loafers. They'll be easier to get in and out of when you're trying on boots."

I hurl myself back down the hall.

"And wipe off that horrid lipstick while you're at it."

Going to the mall with my parents and sisters is about as much fun as cleaning the bathroom. Gary's lucky. He never has to come on these dreary expeditions.

I trail behind the rest of my family, in and out of seven shoe stores. "Why did I have to come anyway?" I complain. "I don't even *want* winter boots."

"I had to come," Susie reminds me, "and I'm not even *getting* new boots 'cause I have to wear *your* old ones."

"Well, bully for you."

In the car April kicks her new, silver-buckled red boots against the seat in front of her. At home she clomps in them up and down the hall. I dump the black pull-ons, which I settled for but won't wear if I can help it, in the vestibule closet.

THAT NIGHT AFTER SUPPER, I sit on the toilet with my pyjama bottoms pooled around my ankles and wrap my arms around my belly. All day it's been like I've been carrying a rock in there. Now it's like my insides are pulling away from me. With Gramma sick, my period has felt much worse somehow. So has not seeing or even hearing from Daniel.

My nose scrinches at the irony smell of my sanitary napkin. Such a stupid thing to call it—a *sanitary napkin,* as if there's anything sanitary about a blood-soaked wad of cotton batting or whatever it is. Careful to avoid the edges, I roll it up. I reach into the cupboard under the sink. That's where Mom keeps used lunch bags—for putting pads into so they can remain a discreet mystery in the wastebasket full of kleenex, Q-tips and balls of hair.

No bags. And nothing in the wastebasket to hide the vile thing under. I know some people wrap them in toilet paper, but Mom says that's wasteful—we aren't made of money. Some people I know flush pads down the toilet, but what if it got stuck part way down? What if Dad had to take apart the pipe to unclog it and found a *sanitary napkin*?

I'll have to go to the kitchen for a bag.

I place the used pad on the floor. It slowly uncurls, exposing the shiny red slick down its middle. I hook a fresh pad into my sanitary belt—another stupid name. I pull up my pyjama bottoms and open the bathroom door.

Gary is in the hall. When he starts for the door, I pull it shut behind me. "Stay out of there. I'm not finished."

"What do you mean, not finished?"

"Never mind. Just wait. I won't be long."

"Well, how do you leave the bathroom when you're *not finished*?" He says it like it's some big joke and follows me to the kitchen. I open a kitchen drawer to a jumble of screws, elastics and old milk caps that Susie used to use when she was having trouble learning number facts. In another drawer are tea towels and pot holders. Lunch bags are here somewhere, I'm sure.

"I hear you're going to the Hallowe'en dance with Blake," Gary says.

"So? What's it to you?"

"He's in my class. I don't like him."

"Then it's good he didn't ask you, isn't it."

"You shouldn't go out with him, Ruby."

"Why? Just because you don't go out with anybody, I shouldn't either? Butt out of my life, why don't you."

"What's the matter in here?" Mom.

"He's bugging me."

"Gary, if you can't say something nice to your sister, don't say anything."

A muscle in Gary's jaw tightens. "All right." He walks stiffly out of the kitchen.

Mom flicks cigarette ash into the sink. "Now—what *are* you doing in here?" She straightens the tea towels I've messed up.

"I can't find lunch bags."

"I'll make your lunch before I go to bed."

I know she doesn't want me to spell out why I need a bag. She has always been in a state of denial about anything to do with menstruation. When I was eleven and showed her this booklet Patty's mother had given her, Mom thumped the iron down beside the ashtray at the end of the ironing board and said, "I don't know what you want to know about that for already." When I found my underwear soaked with blood a few months later, Mom shoved a piece of torn sheet and two safety pins at me and said, "I'll have to get you the proper equipment when your father comes home."

She didn't have *proper equipment* for me then, and now she's being stupid about giving me a bag to dispose of it in.

"Mo-om."

"Oh, for crying out loud." Finally getting it, Mom pulls a grocery bag from the pile folded under the sink. "If you can't find anything else, use one of these." She snaps open the bag.

Clutching the stretched-out-of-shape waistband of my pyjamas, I yank the monstrous bag from Mom's hand and stomp down the hall. Gary steps out of the bathroom. That means he has seen the pad I left on the floor. He glances down at me and turns to go into his bedroom. A pimple on the back of his neck is swollen to a yellow head.

Sometimes life is just disgusting.

ON MY BIRTHDAY, Dad goes to get Gramma and bring her to our house for supper. I haven't seen her since September, and not since we found out she's sick.

"How's my oldest granddaughter?" she asks, sounding like she always has and wrapping me in her usual bear hug. Hugging her back, I can feel her shoulder blades through her blouse.

Doing my best to hide my surprise, I answer, "Fine." She must have been losing weight the last time I saw her, but I didn't notice.

"Sweet sixteen," Dad teases, "and never been kissed?"

"A beauty like this?" Gramma lowers herself gingerly to a chair. "I wouldn't count on it, Ted."

"Don't tell Nan she's a beauty," Mom says. "You'll give her a swollen head."

"Are you kidding? This one is a real doll. Eh, Doll?"

April talks to her macaroni as she eats. Gramma mostly pushes curls of it around her plate. Her appetite hasn't been that good, she says, with the treatments.

After supper, there's a knock on the door. It's Patty.

"Come in," Mom says. "You're just in time for Nan's cake." She lights the candles.

As everyone sings *Happy Birthday*, I think about what to wish for. For Mom to call me Ruby? For Daniel to call, or better yet, move to the city? Or the biggest miracle of all— for Gramma to get better.

"Come on," Susie nags, "blow them out!"

When Mom cuts the cake, I see it's my favourite: confetti cake, with coloured specks all through it. I should have known, from the sprinkles on the icing, that Mom had made the cake I've wanted for my birthday ever since I was old enough to say it.

After cake, I open presents. Gary gives me the Beatles album I've been wanting. *We're Sergeant Pepper's Lonely Hearts Club Band, We hope that you enjoy the show* . . . Susie and April give me a blue leather hair-band. Mom and Dad give me a white turtleneck sweater. Gary says, "That'll be good for hiding hickeys."

Mom looks shocked, and I'm shocked too. Since when does my brother, who as far as I know has never even gone out with a girl, know anything about stuff like that? Is he trying to impress Patty or what?

My present from Gramma is a ceramic figurine. It's an old woman holding a basket of flowers over her arm. There's a little brown sparrow sitting on the edge of the basket. The figurine is in the same style as the balloon man at Gramma's house. She used to take him down off the shelf for me when I was little. She always knew, without me asking, when I wanted to touch him, and she never minded.

"I love this, Gramma. Thank you."

My present from Patty is a ring with tiny red stones in it.

"Ah!" Gary says. "Rubies for the Ruby."

"They aren't real," Patty says, "but I hope you like it."

"I do. It fits, too."

A perfect birthday, I think as I get ready for bed that night. Or it will be, if only my birthday wish comes true. Gramma, please get well.

CHAPTER
TWELVE

THE NIGHT OF THE HALLOWE'EN DANCE, Gary looks at me when we're having supper, but he doesn't say anything. He's in his room when Blake arrives wearing a Swiss cap and lederhosen. He isn't as cute as Daniel was in his Dominion-booth yellow vest, but he looks pretty good. Susie and April take their eyes off *The Beverly Hillbillies* just long enough to say hi.

I glance at the driveway—empty—and Blake cocks his head slightly in the direction of the corner. I introduce him quickly to my parents and to Betty and Frank, over for their weekly game. Mom sets her cigarette in the ashtray she's sharing with Betty, and signals that she wants to see me in the kitchen. I pull my tiger tail behind me and follow her out of the room.

"You didn't mention how old this Blake is," she whispers.

"He's not old. He goes to my school." I don't bother adding that he's in Gary's class but may have flunked once or twice.

"Then he has to be the oldest boy there. Just look at his beard."

"He doesn't have a beard."

"But you can see that if he did, it would be thick, like a man's. Boys that old tend to want things a nice girl like you is *not* prepared to give."

"Mom, we're going to a dance at the school, for Christ sake!" I could point out that if she had just let Daniel stay over that night, I likely would not now be going out with this guy she thinks is too old for me. But why bother.

"Nan, haven't I told you not to use that kind of language in this house?"

"And haven't I told you to call me *Ruby*?" I leave Mom standing in the kitchen. "Goodbye, Mother. We are going to the dance."

"Don't forget to be home by midnight," Dad says.

Blake opens the door of his car and helps me tuck my tail inside. He taps the blackened tip of my nose. "I like your costume."

"Thanks."

At a red light, Blake turns down the DJ on his car radio. "There's this guy, something Larkin, in my class. He wouldn't be your brother or anything, would he?"

"Why?"

"He seems a bit weird."

"He's just quiet, that's all." I hope Blake won't say anything more. I don't want to have to defend my brother. That might make me as weird as him. But surprisingly I don't want Blake bad-mouthing him either. As we pull away from the light, Blake starts telling me about the engine of his car.

Fascinating.

ON THE DANCE FLOOR, even in his Swiss cap and embroidered suspenders, Blake looks pretty cool. Fortunately he's not as unbearably crazy about himself as some good-looking guys are, so I don't feel like too terrible a klutz when I lose the rhythm for a few beats in a Wilson Pickett number. Once, in a slower song, when I step on his foot, Blake makes me stand on his shoes and dances me around the decorated gym like that for the rest of the song.

Some people here tonight I recognize, but so many masks and layers of make-up swirl and bounce around us, it's like I'm out with a whole different crowd from the one that's usually at our school dances. I hope Larry and Keith are here, taking in the fact that Ruby Larkin's little mammary glands are at the dance with Blake Fuller.

Dancing with Blake is not like dancing with Daniel. For one thing, with Daniel I could dance slow songs with my arms around his neck. Blake is so tall I can just reach up to his shoulders. I know I should try not to compare. When I'm with Blake, I probably shouldn't even be thinking about Daniel. *Someone left the cake out in the rain . . .*

Blake bends down over me so my head is closer to his shoulder. But it's hard on his back, he says, so pretty soon he straightens up again. Before the mournful endless song finishes, we move through the other swaying couples to go for a pop.

"What would you like?" Blake asks. "Coke? Ginger ale?"

"Is there any cream soda?"

Blake shudders. "I doubt it. Let's have Coke."

Thirsty in the hot gym, we down our Cokes pretty quick. When we head out again to the dance floor, I've got back a bit of zip. By watching Blake, I find I can do certain moves with my hips I didn't think I could, and somehow, when he holds up my hand to twirl me, my body knows exactly what it's supposed to do.

We make good dance partners, me and Blake. During the slow ones, I'm sure we look pretty cool, even with my tiger tail dragging along behind me, and even if all the blood is draining out of the arm held up to his shoulder.

Part way through *When a Man Loves a Woman*, Blake leans over and wraps his arms around my waist. With my face at his neck I understand Mom was right when she said Blake is older. Not that he stinks, but we've been sweating, and his skin is giving off something definitely male. Back and forth to the music, among headless horsemen, ghosts and goblins, our bodies move in sync.

But then I feel off-kilter—is it the heat of the gym?—as if

my feet might be lifting off the floor.

No, they *are* off the floor! Blake is straightening up and lifting me with him!

"Too hard on my back," he murmurs into my ear. My arms fit easily around his neck now. My legs—I don't know if he did this with them or I did—are wrapped around Blake's waist.

"There," he says.

It's so much like how my dad would have held me when I was little, I start to laugh. Then suddenly it's funny but not funny ha-ha, what I'm feeling. Actually it's not even funny, it's ridiculous. Blake is holding me like this to save his back, not to make me horny, but horny is what I am. Being this close to him, my legs wide apart, wearing just the tights of my tiger-suit, and my underwear of course . . . most very definitely!

"Can you put me down?" I say. "I can't do this."

Blake lowers me to the floor. "Can't do what?"

"I don't know. Dance like that."

We go back to dancing as we did earlier, Blake upright, only now instead of reaching up to his shoulder, I slip my arm under his and let my hand rest near his shoulder blade. He has muscles there Daniel didn't have. And where Blake's hands touch my back now, they feel bigger and warmer than before. I'd like to put my face close to his neck again, catch that smell of him, but won't ask him to bend over and certainly not to pick me up again.

Maybe it wasn't there before, or maybe I've just become conscious of it, as Percy Faith wails on and Blake rocks with me slowly around our little corner of the dance floor. The length of Blake's thigh near my crotch. Occasionally even touching. Now that I am aware of it, it's almost worse than when he was carrying me. With each bar of music, it seems, I want to . . . not really, but it occurs to me that I could . . . press myself against Blake's thigh.

My arm is getting heavy. I let my hand fall to Blake's waist. Blake places my other hand, the one he has been holding, around his waist too. When he wraps his arms around my shoulders, my face is hot next to his chest, and again I feel the movement of his thigh against me.

And again.

Somehow, we have made our way over to the line of jack-o-lanterns along the bleachers. The other dancers, I realize, are no longer near us. With the gentlest pressure, Blake's thigh moves against me, and in the corner of the gym, there is no question I want nothing more than to press myself to it.

At the end of the bleachers Blake turns slowly, backs himself up against the wall, and pulls me to him. He slides down the wall a bit so he's not so much taller than me. Without my having to bend my legs at all, his thigh is exactly right. With one hand Blake gently lifts my chin and kisses me.

I wondered, before, if he would want to kiss me good-night. I wondered if I would let him. Or not. But I never imagined so *wanting* him to kiss me. Wanting him to, not just because it's nice if a guy wants to kiss you, but because where his thigh is pressing . . . or maybe it's me pressing, or maybe both of us . . . it feels so good, and necessary . . . and our mouths are so wet, and in a moment . . .

Oh God, oh my God . . . what I have made happen alone in my bed, it could happen. Here. Holding his thigh between . . . That sweet explosion could . . . with Blake. Here, in the dark corner of the gym.

"Come on, you two, out of there." My history teacher, with her arms crossed, glares at us till we move past her out of the corner. "Ruby Larkin, I didn't expect this kind of behaviour from you."

Neither did I, Miss Parker, neither did I.

I want to push myself out of Blake's arms, run from the gym and never come back. But Blake holds me and says, "That was beautiful, Ruby."

"I'm sorry. I . . ."

He smiles down at me. "Don't be."

CHAPTER
THIRTEEN

TREES SCRATCH THE SKY with their hard, bare branches. Every morning frost coats the lawns and roofs. The temperature plunges lower.

On the way home from school Patty natters on to me about how badly she did on our geography test. I'm too bored to do more than pretend to listen. It's early in the season yet for ice, but at the side of the road, puddles have solidified. Why is it, I wonder, that some puddles don't freeze at all, some freeze solid right through, and some form a thin layer of ice above the frozen puddle below, a big bubble of air in between?

Step by slow step my sneakers crunch through the fragile crystal layers. I love the sound of their breaking. Tink! The first break in the surface. Crack! As the breaks grow. Crunch! Beneath my feet pressing on the broken pieces.

When there is no more clink and pop, when the sound is no more than a muffled crunch beneath the soles of my shoes, I move on to the next frozen puddle. It's the same every winter, but each time I do it, it feels surprising, like it's my first time.

One night, after April is asleep and Susie has gone to bed with a book—she's so pleased with the new bed-light she got for her birthday—Mom fusses around as she always does on the rare occasion she and Dad are going out. She instructs Gary to take good care of us, as if I need to be taken care of.

When finally my parents have left for their Couples' Club at the church, I turn on the TV and curl up on the chesterfield to watch my favourite show, which Mom, of course, hates.

Soon Gary is leaning against the doorway of the living room. "What are you doing?"

"Watching *Ben Casey*."

"Did I say you could?"

I don't bother to answer.

Gary comes over and leans his face down in front of me. "Did I say you could watch *Ben Casey*? What if I want to watch something else?"

I flick my brother away. He doesn't want to watch TV. Since his friend Wayne took a job up north a year ago, Gary never does anything normal like watch TV, go to parties or hang around at the mall. He spends hours in his room, copying weather maps out of the newspaper into a notebook. Since Gramma's been sick, he's been doing it even more.

I stare at the TV, where Ben Casey is pressing what look like instruments of torture against the sole of a patient's foot, but the patient doesn't seem to feel anything. Finally Gary leaves the room.

Toward the end of the show, the woman with nerveless feet is walking on the beach. She doesn't notice she has cut herself on a piece of broken glass. "You will have to be more careful," Ben Casey tells her as he wraps a bandage around her foot, and the show ends.

What would that be like, I wonder, to feel nothing in part of your body? To not know your skin was being cut or burned, touched or kissed?

In the hall, Gary steps out of his room. "What are you doing?"

"What's it to you?"

"Come here."

"Why should I?"

"I'm sorry I bugged you about your show."

I shrug and as I move to pass him, Gary grabs my arm. "Come here."

"What?"

He turns me to face him. We're so close I can see the separate threads in the plaid pattern of his shirt. It occurs to me, but it's too weird—Gary's never been *this* weird—that he could, with those slobbery lips of his . . . kiss me. It's as if, almost . . . he might even want to.

I push my hands up between us. "Don't, Gary."

"Don't what?"

"I don't know. Whatever you're doing."

"I just wanted to say I was sorry."

"Well, you did. Now leave me alone."

Gary drops his hands. They dangle at his sides. Again I get this feeling he wants something.

I step past him into my room and close the door. I lean my back against it. My heart is pounding.

After a while, with the quietest *snick,* Gary's door closes too.

I cross my room then, pull back the curtain from my window and look out. Soft rectangles of light shine through the curtains of houses on the street behind ours.

Things with Gary used to be so simple. There's a picture of us somewhere, taken when he was heading off to school one day when I was about three. We're in the vestibule: I'm wearing my boots and my pyjamas, and Gary, with a book under his arm, is leaning over so I can kiss him goodbye. And there was that time Mom first left us alone with Gary in charge, the time he took me to the ravine with his friends. Hours after we got back home, Mom was still insisting Gary tell her where we had gone. As far as I know, he never told. My protector from his friend with the beer and then from Mom.

I let the curtain fall across my reflection in the black window of my bedroom.

I don't know when I stopped adoring Gary. But that look on his face tonight—it was like his eyes were pleading with me. Probably not with desire like I thought at first, but maybe with *Please like me; I need someone to like me.*

I know what that's like. And with Wayne gone, and if Gramma doesn't beat this cancer thing—and sometimes I can actually admit that this is possible—maybe there'll be nobody around any more who really *likes* Gary. I used to think Mom did, till he told me about her not wanting him to be a carpenter. And there *is* this disgusted look she gives him when he asks her sometimes if something's wrong. She might even, if it's possible, not like Gary even more than she doesn't like me.

I've at least got Patty. And Blake. April, I guess, too. Remembering how Gary looked almost admiring the day I told everyone to call me Ruby, and remembering how he stuck up for me about going to the Ex to meet Daniel, I think that maybe Gary likes me too. But what if Gary really has nobody? I turn on my radio to fill my head with music, but what's playing is too sweet and cheerful, so I turn it off again.

When Mom and Dad come home from Couples' Club, it's with big news. Frank has a new job out west. He and Betty are moving before the end of the year.

"Poor Betty," Mom says, "she won't know a soul out there."

Funny, I was just thinking about Gary being alone, and now Mom will soon be without Betty. Poor Betty? Poor Mom.

"Why doesn't Betty just tell Frank she doesn't want to move?" I ask. It seems so obvious.

Mom's laugh reminds me of Betty's, husky and with a slightly bitter edge. "You'll understand some day, Nan. That's just not the way things work when you're married."

THE NEXT AFTERNOON, taking a break from my homework, I come into the kitchen for a glass of water. Dad is saying, "You'll have to this time."

Mom answers, "I don't know if I can."

Dad leaves the room. He looks almost angry.

"Can what?" I ask.

Mom fiddles with the cigarette package on the table in front of her. "Never mind." She opens the flap of the package, but it's empty.

Knowing how she must be feeling about Betty's move on top of Gramma being sick, I actually for a moment feel sorry for her. I go to the cupboard to get her a new pack from her carton, but there isn't one. "Are you out of cigarettes?"

"Do you see cigarettes in the cupboard? No. There are no cigarettes in the cupboard. I guess that means I'm out of them, doesn't it?"

Taking off down the hall I mutter, "Pardon me for living."

Turns out Mom is supposed to be quitting. She's going into hospital next week for some kind of surgery. Something about her arteries being clogged up after so many years of cigarettes. Being at home with her is harder than ever, so I spend as much time as I can with Patty or Blake. Parked in his car among the trees by the creek, I like what he makes me feel.

"Patty," I ask in her room on Monday after school, "how far do you go with Ray?"

"Ruby, are you and Blake . . . ?"

"Mm, no."

"But it's starting to feel like a good idea?"

"I don't know."

"Well, Babe, just let me say, be careful. It feels way more complicated than I thought it would be."

"So you and Ray . . . ?"

Patty just smiles.

"My God, talk about the cat who swallowed the canary!"

"What?"

I bash Patty over the head with her pillow.

Kathy Stinson

When I get home, Mom is in her armchair watching *The Secret Storm*, her feet tucked underneath her. Smoke from a cigarette sifts through her hair.

"I just got one pack," she says. "Just to get me through to when I have to go in."

CHAPTER
FOURTEEN

WITH MOM AWAY, the house feels different in a way that's hard to describe. It's like there's more room here, more light. But it's like no one—except Gary, who's in his room most of the time lately anyway—knows quite how to *be* here without her. Susie and April don't squabble. They play nicely together in their room. Dad isn't bustling around in his workshop or fixing something around the house all the time. He sits in the living room more, just reading the paper with his feet up on the hassock.

One night I flip the channels through all the possibilities, but there's nothing on. I click off the TV. Dad lowers the newspaper to his lap.

"It's odd with your mother not here, isn't it."

"Mhm." I flop into the empty armchair. "Did it hurt—the operation Mom had?"

"I'm sure it was no picnic, but she was under anaesthetic

during surgery, and she's on lots of painkillers now."

"Can I go see her next time you go in? Visitors over twelve are allowed. I called the hospital and asked."

"You know your mother said she doesn't want you or Gary to see her there, Ruby. Hospitals aren't very happy places."

"I know."

"Do you miss her, Ruby?"

I shrug. It's Gramma I miss. We've talked on the phone a few times, but Mom says her last visit here tired her out, she needs her rest. "Do you?"

"You know, your mother and I haven't been apart overnight in—let's see—close to twenty years. Except when she was in hospital to have you kids."

"Really?"

"Remember how excited you were when Susie turned out to be a girl?"

I smile. "I thought you and Mom picked a girl baby because I wanted a little sister so badly."

"Yes, and then it was Susie's turn to be excited when April was born." Dad drops his newspaper to the floor. "Your brother was pretty excited when you were born too, you know."

From under my long bangs I eye Dad with suspicion.

"He was, and you were very close when you were kids. You'll be good friends again once you're both done all your growing up. You'll see." Dad lowers his feet to the floor. "Did I ever tell you how your Uncle Dave and I scrapped when we were teenagers? He almost put me through a window once."

"Dad, I don't think you and Dave is the same as me and Gary." I pick up an empty ashtray from the coffee table, run a finger over its smooth glass edge.

"No, I guess it's not."

"But we're not exactly *not* friends now," I tell Dad. It occurs to me, though, that Gary hasn't spoken to me since the night I told him to leave me alone.

"Good. That's good."

Maybe Gary did want to kiss me that night, like it seemed for a second that he did. Maybe that's why I'm still feeling as awkward about talking to him as he is about talking to me. I just don't know.

I place the ashtray back on the table. "Do you think she'll quit?"

"Doctor says she has to."

Dad talks for a while, about how they both used to smoke and tried to quit together a few times, how it worked for him but not for her. He talks about when they first met, at a dance, and where they bought their first house. He talks about why he likes being a plumber and running his own business.

Through it all, I lean forward, elbows on my knees. "You've never talked to me like this before."

"Guess there hasn't been the chance, somehow." Dad sighs. "You know, Ruby," he says, "you're a good listener. Do you think of using that at all some day? You'd be good at—well, you know—any of those jobs where the main thing is being able to listen."

The phone rings. It's Blake. I talk for a minute then hang up.

"Boyfriend?" Dad asks.

"Yeah." I plunk myself on the chesterfield. "I told him I was talking to you."

For a moment neither of us has anything to say.

"You like this fellow quite a lot?" Dad asks.

"In a way, yeah."

"I gathered, from what I walked in on downstairs the other day."

"Da-ad!"

"I hope you don't spend all your time smooching."

"We listen to music too," I say. It's a scramble to come up with anything else Blake and I do. "And talk," I say, although I can't at the moment think of anything Blake and I have ever really talked about.

"That's good. It's good to talk. To talk . . . and listen." Dad hesitates, then goes on. "That other fellow . . ." He crosses his arms across his chest. "He was nice, wasn't he? The one I drove home that time. Daniel, I think his name was?"

I swallow. The skin of my cheeks prickles.

"Did he just call you the once after that night?"

I close my eyes to stop the diamond pattern in the carpet from swirling. Daniel called? He . . . I didn't . . . Nobody . . .

I face Dad squarely and push the words out. "Dad, nobody ever told me Daniel called." I see him piecing together what must have happened. The call, taken by Mom, and—

"I'm sorry. I shouldn't have brought it up. You probably haven't thought about him in weeks. What with Blake and all."

I pick up the ashtray from the table again. "You know what, Dad?" I shift its weight back and forth between my hands. "I still think about Daniel every day."

Dad gently removes the ashtray from my hands. He places it back on the table.

My throat tightens. "What *is* it with her?"

Dad stares toward the window. Across the road, the swings hang empty. It seems Dad's going to say something that might explain everything.

"I don't know, Ruby. She wasn't always like this. It wasn't till we'd . . ."—it's like this is just occurring to him—"till we'd been married a couple of years . . . that she started to . . . change."

"With her, everything I do—or even *want*—is wrong." I pick up Mom's cigarette lighter now, repeatedly flick the ignitor.

Dad looks suddenly old. "I know. Believe me, I know." The lines around his eyes are so deep I can't believe I've never noticed them before. "But she does love you."

The flint catches beneath my thumb. Flame bursts from the lighter. At the same moment the telephone rings.

"Careful there." Dad goes to answer it this time.

When he comes back, he perches on the hassock, arms resting on his knees. "Your mother wants me to bring a few things to the hospital when I go in tomorrow."

Part of me wants Dad to go back to talking about how Mom loves me. Except, if not telling me when Daniel called is how she shows it, then really, what's the point? "I guess I should go see if I finished my homework."

Dad nods. When I stand to go, he gets up too. "Ah, geez, Ruby."

He doesn't have any more words, it seems, but he wraps his arms around me, cups his hand around my head and holds it to his chest. He doesn't seem to mind that I'm getting his shirt wet.

THE NEXT DAY Dad is running late. I've already started supper when he comes in from his last call, grumbling about having to go out on one more because he can't put this leaky pipe off another day. And he still has to get in to see Mom.

"Can you hold off supper a bit?" he says. "Make your sisters some Kraft Dinner if they can't wait."

"'Kay."

"And Ruby—" He fishes in his pocket. "Here's the list of things your mother wants. If you could put them together in a bag for me, I'll take them to the hospital as soon as I finish with this pipe."

I put the potatoes in cold water, rinse my hands, and reach under the sink for a bag for Mom's things.

My parents' room is a part of the house I never go into. I don't think I was ever told not to go in there, but something about it has always given me a No-Trespassing kind of feeling. Maybe because of the bogey man I saw in the corner when I went in once when I was little, after I had a bad dream. I couldn't see it all that well as I debated which of my parents to waken, but the bogey man was green, had a crooked frown, and its eye looked like it was ripped open and dripping down. Its scrunched-up body was much smaller than its head. He was so scary I scurried right back to bed without telling anyone about my bad dream.

All that's in the corner now is a small wooden chair over which are hanging the shirts Dad has worn since Mom went to hospital. Beside it, on the floor, is an old green cushion. The curtains are drawn across the window and the bed is unmade. A staleness hangs in the air, a smell of old tobacco smoke and unwashed laundry.

I flick on the bed lamp closest to the dresser.

Moisturizing cream, nail file, crossword puzzle book. All these are on top of Mom's night stand. I put them into the bag.

A nightgown, three pairs of underpants—those will be in her dresser.

Inside a top drawer are socks and underwear. Six pairs of black, navy or white ankle socks. Six pairs of plain cotton briefs—four white and two beige—I guess she applies her thing about *nice girls don't wear black underwear* to herself too; it's not just part of her plot to keep me pure. And two white brassieres with lacy cups.

It surprises me, the lace. Does it turn Dad on—not now, but back when they were young enough for sex, did it—to see Mom's breasts all wrapped in lace? Did he used to fondle them the way Blake has started fondling mine, under my sweater but over my bra—plain cotton, of course? Did Mom like it?

Get real, Ruby.

As I fold Mom's underpants into the bag, I notice on the wall beside the dresser a photo of my parents on their wedding day, a different shot from the one in the dining room. She probably wore a lacy bra back then too. My eyes linger on the photo, not because I expect to see my mother's underwear in it, but because I've never seen a full-length picture of her dress before. The one in the dining room is just a head-and-shoulders shot.

It's quite fitted across the bodice, which is beaded, and has long sleeves with the same beads at the wrists. Something about the line of the dress around Mom's waist makes it look . . . thick maybe? It almost makes me think . . . Impossible! *My mother* pregnant on her wedding day? I quickly do the math with Gary's birth date. I was right, she wasn't. She couldn't have been. Unless . . . what if she had a miscarriage? Did my parents *have* to get married? I study the photo again. Surely not.

The next drawer—I'm here to do a job, not investigate my parents' past—contains shirts, and the next shorts and slacks. In the bottom drawer I find her nightgowns. On top is a plaid flannel one I've often seen her wearing under her turquoise housecoat. I take it from the drawer, fold it on top of the other things in the bag, and check the list. That's it. Done.

I've barely been breathing, I realize, and allow myself to exhale deeply.

When I go to close the bottom drawer, I see another familiar nightgown, covered in tiny pink and purple flowers. Would she rather have that one in the hospital? It is prettier. But what do I care what she wears? I don't. And after what she did about Daniel, I'm never going to care about anything to do with her again. But I take the plaid nightgown out of the bag and replace it with the flowered one. As I'm putting the plaid one back in the drawer, something underneath the next nightgown, an older pale yellow one, catches my eye. A bit of something red.

I've got what Dad asked me to get, so I have no reason to go poking around, but carefully I lift the nightgowns onto the dresser. I take up the red nightie—it's very small—and sit down on the side of my parents' bed. I feel between my fingers the silky, filmy material, and jump up, suddenly uncomfortable with where I'm sitting.

I know from the wedding photos that Mom was really good-looking when she was younger, but she can't ever have worn this. Not even back then. Can she? Maybe Dad gave it to her as a joke.

But wow, does it ever feel nice. And what a great shade of red.

Before putting the little nightie back in the drawer, I hold it up against my body. Through the filmy material, I can see the pattern of my sweater and the buckle of my jeans. The ruffled hem falls just below my crotch. The matching neckline, I see when I pull the nightie on over my clothes, is very low. Not that it much matters. Even where it covers me, this thing wouldn't hide anything.

Looking in the mirror, I try to imagine how I'd look without all my other clothes on. The swell of my breasts, which I swear are getting bigger since I started seeing Blake—responding to all his attention? My dark nipples holding the sheer film of fabric out from the rest of my skin, all glowy-red underneath it. Wouldn't I just love to wear something like this for Blake? He would reach for me and hold the silky material against my skin and kiss me through it, all over, and when he got . . .

Quickly I take the thing off. I have no business wearing it. I no longer have any business being in this room. Carefully I place the little red nightie in the bottom of the drawer, cover it with Mom's real nightgowns, and close the drawer. I fold over the top of the paper bag, ready for Dad to take to the hospital.

There *is* one other drawer. A small drawer beside Mom's sock and underwear drawer. I didn't bother to open it before because I knew it was too small to hold nightgowns, but I wonder, now, what is in it. What other little surprises might Mom have hidden away?

It's none of my business.

Really.

But why should I worry about her privacy if she never bothers to worry about what matters to me?

Maybe I shouldn't worry. But Dad will be home soon anyway. A leaky pipe isn't usually a big job. I take the bag of Mom's things to the kitchen.

AFTER DAD COMES IN from his call and has gone out again to the hospital, and once my sisters are watching TV, I drain some of the water off the potatoes, flick the heat on under the pot, and go back down the hall. I wasn't planning to, exactly, but I seem to have decided somehow that April and Susie can wait to eat till Dad gets home. Once again I find myself standing in front of Mom's dresser. The small drawer beside her underwear drawer is open.

Inside it are old make-up, hair barrettes, a scarf. A little jewellery box. Nothing much.

All the jewellery in the box I have seen before. A couple of metal and coloured-stone brooches, a string of beads, a bracelet that looks like half a handcuff. There are a couple of matchbooks in the box too. They look really old. One is from a restaurant in Niagara Falls, the other from a hotel there. Is that where my parents had their honeymoon? I've never asked and they've never said.

There are some papers under the jewellery box. Pretty boring. A couple of old bills for things around the house, a first-aid article clipped from a magazine. What did I expect? Papers saying I'm adopted, I'm not really my mother's daughter at all? I unfold another article—*Five-Day Plan To Quit Smoking*, dated nine years ago. And then another stop-smoking thing, dated a few years later.

I always figured Mom smoked because she liked it, but if she's been trying to quit for this long, she must hate that she can't. Maybe that's why she tries to keep such a tight grip on everything I do—*can't control myself so I'll control my daughter instead.*

Maybe I ought to take up smoking. Wouldn't that just rot her little white ankle socks?

Flipping through the last of the papers, I come to a card made of pink construction paper. Printed on the front in purple and blue crayon is *Happy Mother's Day!* A line of yellow and red tulips marches across the bottom. Inside, *Dear Mommy, I love you. Hugs and kisses from Nanny.*

I made her this sweet card. Judging by the formation of the letters, I was just barely able to print.

And Mom kept it.

Under the card there's a Normal School certificate for Joan Gibbons. Isn't Normal School what they used to call Teachers' College? Mom told me once how a long time ago married women weren't allowed to teach, but she never mentioned anything about wanting to herself. I never knew.

There's a louder than usual shriek from the living room, and a sudden wailing. The music from Gary's room gets louder. He mustn't catch me here, snooping. Blood rushes to my head. Quickly I duck behind my parents' bed, dizzy.

But it's not like I've taken anything. I *did* have to come in to get Mom's things. And there's nothing important here anyway. Still, when my sisters are quiet, when Gary's music is again muffled by his closed door, and after my heart goes back to beating normally, the old bogey-man feeling returns.

When I start to put things back in the drawer the way I found them, I notice, sticking out from under the little jewellery box, the corner of a photograph. I'm ashamed of the snooping I've been doing, but not ashamed enough to stop myself from slipping it from the pile.

It's an old black and white photo. Of a man. Why isn't it with all the other photos, in the box in the hall cupboard?

Whoever the man is, his arm folded as he leans back against some old-fashioned car, he's very good looking. And boy, does he look a lot like Mom. His hair is thick and dark. And something around the eyes . . .

I turn the photo over. Nothing written on the back.

He looks quite young, maybe twenty, maybe not even. But with no date, that doesn't tell me much, especially since I don't know anything about cars. But this man— geez, he looks so much like Mom they might be, they *must* be related. Could my mother have had . . . a brother? A brother who maybe died soon after this photo was taken?

But why would I never have heard her even speak of him?

I know—because he didn't die. They had an enormous fight. And that's why there are no pictures of him in the box of family photos. It also explains why Mom is always so anxious about me and Gary getting along. Because she's afraid we could end up like her and her brother, never seeing each other, never speaking.

I glance at my watch. Almost six. Dad will be home soon, and I've still got the rest of supper to get ready. I have to put this photo back in the drawer and bury it as it has been buried possibly for longer than I've been alive.

Could I really have an uncle out there somewhere? Does he even know I exist?

The smell of something burning hits me halfway up the hall. The potatoes. I yank them off the element. The pot has boiled dry. Its bottom is crusty and black. I scoop the unburned parts of the potatoes into a bowl, but the scorched smell is all through them. I dump them in the garbage, quickly peel more, and cut them into small pieces that will cook quickly.

If Mom hated her brother so much she never once in all my life even mentioned him, it's weird she'd keep a photo of him. And if Gramma had a son, wouldn't she have mentioned him, even if Mom wouldn't?

I flick on the oven and lay frozen fish sticks on a pan.

Maybe the man in the picture isn't a brother at all. I try to think of his face again.

The man's eyes—is this right? I think so—they're looking out of the picture as if . . . I should have thought of this before. As if he is mad-crazy about whoever is holding the camera.

Mom?

Could this be . . . ?

An old boyfriend! It must be! An old boyfriend Mom never got over, and that's why she still has his picture. Yes!

Why else would she keep a photo of a man where no one else would ever see it—unless he was someone she cared about a lot and someone no one was supposed to know about? I bet *he's* the one who gave her that red nightie. What if—oh, man—what if it was *his* baby and not Dad's that she was pregnant with when she got married? If she was. Goose bumps flit down my arms.

I get cutlery from the drawer, set the table, then put the extra knife and fork away again.

Whether she was pregnant or not, if Mom loved this man enough to keep his picture all these years, why would she marry Dad? Because . . . maybe . . . this other guy dumped her?

No. You wouldn't want a picture of a guy who'd hurt you. Maybe he moved away, too far for them to go on seeing each other. Or else it was a summer thing. Like, it seems—but I can't bear to admit it—me and Daniel.

Maybe Mom and this guy wanted to get married, but her parents said they were too young and wouldn't let them see each other any more. It's hard to believe Gramma would be like that, but maybe she wasn't so mellow when Mom was a girl, or maybe Poppa was more strict?

Whatever the reason, could it be that if Mom couldn't have her own true love, she's not going to let me have mine either? So she doesn't tell me when he calls? Maybe she even tells him not to call again.

I run water into the burnt pot and pick at the chunks of potato stuck to its bottom. But the black is burnt on so tight, it's going to have to soak.

I'm going to have to try calling Daniel again. Will he still want to talk to me?

I stab at a potato with a fork. The steam scalds my hand. I run it under the cold water tap. Then, dumping a bag of frozen peas into a pot, I spill half of them on the floor. Furiously, I chase them around the kitchen, trying to catch them on the dustpan with the broom.

"I'm hungry," April whines, tugging on the hem of my shirt.

I snap at her. "We'll eat when Dad gets home."

April turns and runs from the kitchen.

"April, wait." I drop the broom, catch April in the hall and scoop her up in my arms. "I'm sorry. Do you have rumblies in your tummy? Do you need a cracker to chase them away?"

When Dad gets home, my sister is sitting on my lap, happily munching her cracker, and tears are streaming down my face.

"Is something burning?"

"I burned the potatoes. And the pot."

"Don't worry. It's just an old pot."

I nod, but can't stop crying.

"Honey, what is it?"

I just shake my head.

"Ruby?"

I lift April down from my lap. "Go tell Susie and Gary supper's almost ready."

"Your mother's going to be fine, Ruby."

Dad means after her surgery. He means her body will go on working properly now that the doctors have unclogged her arteries.

But can you ever be fine if in your heart you love someone you can't be with? Or if you really want to do something with your life and never get to?

CHAPTER
FIFTEEN

GRAMMA'S CANCER ISN'T RESPONDING to treatment. I haven't seen her since my birthday. I miss her. The doctors are prescribing stronger medications to be taken more often, but it doesn't look good. Mom—home from hospital for three days now without a cigarette but only out of bed to go to the bathroom—has an old lover in her dresser, along with an out-of-date teaching certificate, a sexy nightie, and a faded Happy Mother's Day card. There's been no answer, lately, when I've tried Daniel's phone. Gary and I still aren't talking. Susie's over at a friend's, and April—I have to love her—wants me to read her a story. She loves to join in on the line, "The sky is falling, the sky is falling!" It's almost as if she knows.

When order has been restored in Henny Penny's kingdom, April says, "Play cut-outs with me now?"

We dress the paper dolls and put them in April's bus. "Where are we going today?" I ask.

"To the zoo." April starts to move the bus away from the line-up of dolls on the step.

"Wait," I say, crawling across the floor. "Davy and Heidi want to go too."

"They can't. They were bad."

"Really? What did they do?"

"Heidi wet her bed. And Davy said a bad word."

Poor April. She's been wetting her bed again lately, and Mom's not sympathetic.

"Maybe Heidi can't help it," I suggest.

"It's still bad."

"Tell me—what bad word did Davy say?"

April looks at me from under a shock of dark hair. Down the hall, Mom's bedroom door is open. April whispers, "Shit."

"That's a great one, isn't it?"

April's eyes open wide, hardly believing her big sister would say such a thing. "Maybe Davy should do what I used to do when I wanted to say bad words."

"What?"

I bury my mouth in the crook of my elbow. "You do it too."

She does.

I whisper, "Shit shit shit."

April giggles. She tries to whisper "shit shit shit" into her elbow, but can't stop giggling.

Soon I'm giggling too.

Mom calls out, "What are you two laughing about out there?"

"Nothing," I tell her.

"Nan, will you get April some lunch please?"

"'Kay."

The cut-outs are left to get to the zoo on their own.

"How come Mom always calls you Nan?" April asks, following me out to the kitchen.

"I guess she can't help it."

"Just like Heidi can't help sometimes wetting her bed?"

"Something like that, yeah." I spread peanut butter on enough bread to make sandwiches for us both. While April is finishing her second half—she is such a slow eater—I go downstairs to start some laundry. I never do it when Mom is up and around, but there's getting to be quite a stack.

The smell of urine permeates the heap of sheets. It reminds me of once when I peed on purpose, with all my clothes on, when I was little. The question of what it would be like to do that had just popped into my head from nowhere, and instead of lifting the lid of the toilet, I sat up on top of it, fully dressed, and peed.

It was pleasantly hot, I remember, the pee soaking my underwear and shorts, pooling around my thighs. And I loved the secret sound it made—*shshsh*.

But then it was running over the smooth white seat and

trickling down my legs, and soon there was a puddle of pee beside the toilet. A very yellow puddle with rivers creeping along the floor toward the bathtub. The lace-edged ankles of my socks were wet, and my sneakers left footprints as I tried to back away from the puddle. I knew I had to clean up the mess I'd made and was wiping the floor with my shorts when Dad called in, "Are you okay, honey?"

It was good Mom was at the hospital getting a new baby, I remember thinking, because I knew Dad wouldn't open the door on me like she would. "I'm okay, Daddy," I said. "I just had an accident." He wouldn't spank me either.

When I came out of the bathroom, a towel wrapped around me and my clothes bunched in a ball, my dad said, "Put those downstairs in the laundry room, Nan. Mommy will wash them when she comes home."

All these years later I can still feel the smile I swallowed behind my lips that day. Was I pleased because I'd got away with my little experiment? Or because Mom would have to suffer its consequences? Was there some funny kind of tension between us even that long ago?

April calls from the top of the stairs, "I'm done my sandwich."

I wipe her hands and face and take her to her room for a nap. She doesn't sleep in the afternoon any more, but still lies down with her books and teddy for a while after lunch. Mom is sleeping today too. The only sounds in the house are the muffled patter of some radio DJ behind Gary's bedroom door and the rhythmic sloshing of the washing machine downstairs.

It makes a couple of jerky choking noises, and I start down to move the sheets into the dryer, but the washer is filling with water again. They still have to rinse.

Maybe this would be a good time to try talking to Gary. Except I'm still not sure what I want to say to him exactly.

I can't call Gramma because she always sleeps after lunch now. But I've also been wanting to try reaching Daniel again. I could do that while the laundry is rinsing.

In the kitchen the phone rings.

It's Blake. He wants to take me to the school dance next weekend. It will be the five-week anniversary of our first date. Thinking of being with him—my hand curled around the receiver after we've said goodbye—my belly fills with a naughty sort of tingle not that different from what I felt when I was little and decided to pee my pants on purpose.

Out of the corner of my eye I see Gary standing in the doorway of the kitchen. When I hang up he says, "You be careful, Ruby."

CHAPTER
SIXTEEN

"BOYS WITH CARS ARE DANGEROUS," Mom says, her hands deep in the hot dishwater for the first time since coming home. "And Blake isn't even a boy, he's a man. You're just a girl."

And will be for the rest of my life if you have your way. I wipe dry a grey melmac plate. Things would have been so much simpler if Mom had just stayed in bed, or hadn't found out about Blake's car. "But, Mom—"

"I don't like you seeing him, Nan. Boys with cars expect things. Especially boys as old as this one."

"Mom, you're impossible. Even if you don't trust Blake, don't you trust me?"

"Trust has nothing to do with it."

"It's not like Blake just *got* the car. And I've been in it with him lots of times before and—"

"But you lied to me."

"I didn't."

"There are lies of *commission* and lies of *omission*. Not telling me you were going out in Blake's car was a lie of omission."

I wipe the next plate in furious circles. "So you've lied to me too then, haven't you?"

Mom's back straightens slightly. Her hands drip dishwater on the edge of the counter. "What do you mean?"

"A *lie of omission*?" I hug the plate to my chest, hardly believing I'm going to confront her on this. "Not telling me when Daniel called?"

A crimson stain creeps up the side of Mom's neck. The set of her jaw makes clear she is not about to answer my accusation.

"You're not going to stop me seeing Blake too." I bash the plate onto the stack in the cupboard. "I am going—with him—to this dance."

Mom swirls her hand around the sink full of water and pulls the plug. "All right. As long as it's in a group," she says. "I don't want you dating him alone."

I could laugh. As if being in a group makes a difference. As if nothing happens behind closed bedroom doors at parties, on the way to and from dances, at church drop-ins or anywhere else kids go in groups. I would laugh, but don't need to. I have won.

I hang the dish towel—neatly—on its bar.

AS IT TURNS OUT, the dance is nothing special. The band isn't much good and there are too many teacher chaperones. Blake and I leave early.

Blake steers with one hand as we leave the school parking lot. I snuggle into his side. Our headlights pierce the night, bounce from lamp post to lamp post and across cars parked by the curb for the night. Thump—thump—thump. The music of the dance band still thrums and rings in my head.

Blake pulls the car into a dead end near the ravine at the far end of the park. He cuts the lights and the engine. As we kiss, I let the tip of my tongue touch Blake's upper lip. I love knowing how much my being here would scandalize my mother if she knew.

Slowly Blake's hand, on my knee, begins to slide up. The blonde hairs on the back of his hand glow in the light from a distant streetlight. My own hand, resting on Blake's thigh, squeezes the muscle of it, firm and long beneath my fingers. Blake's mouth wraps itself over mine and we neck like we have so many times now.

Then I feel his thumb move off my leg. It is sliding, gently, against the zipper of my jeans.

We have never done below-the-waist stuff before. But under my hand he is shifting his leg. He wants me to do to him what he is doing to me.

I have wondered, alone in my bed at night, what that would be like. To touch with my hand where I have felt his jeans lump

against me. Thump—thump—thump. Music reverberating
in my head still? Or my heart pounding against my chest?

My fingers shift. The tips of them find Blake's denim-
bound erection, and slowly I allow the length of my fingers
and the palm of my hand to cover the entire firm mound of
it. Through Blake's jeans I think I can feel the ridge of his
penis-head. Is he wearing underwear, or is there just the one
layer of cloth between my skin and his? And have I been
dancing with him all night, and other nights too maybe,
with so little between us?

Into Blake's neck I whisper, "What's it like?"

"What?"

"You know." I apply a gentle pressure to the lump in his
jeans. "What's it look like?"

He pulls in a shallow breath. "What do you want me to
say, Ruby? It's . . . I don't know."

"Can I see it? I never have. Seen one I mean."

"You're kidding me, right?"

"Well, I saw my brother's once when I opened his
bedroom door on Christmas morning about five years ago
'cause when I knocked I thought he said to come in, but—"

"No," Blake says. "I meant . . . about seeing it."

"Oh. Sorry. I'm sorry. I shouldn't have asked. It was a
dumb idea."

"It's okay. I don't mind. I just . . ." Blake laughs a nervous
laugh. "No one's ever asked me if they could *see it* before."

"Well I guess I'm not *like* anyone else, am I?"

Blake stares into the windshield. He takes a deep breath and unbuckles his belt. In spite of the cool night, the air inside the car feels suddenly warm. The radio, on low, plays a slow sexy tune I don't recognize.

Blake unsnaps the waistband of his jeans. The teeth of his zipper separate, and from the opening in his pants it springs. Big. White like chicken skin in the darkness of the car. It is nothing like the penis on the health charts at school. It has veins. Its mushroom cap is shiny and dark. Blake is holding his breath. So am I.

"Touch me, Ruby."

In the tear-drop hole in the end of Blake's turkey-neck of a penis, something glistens. A single droplet. It just sits there, and it's just a single drop, but I know—suddenly—that I am not ready for where we're headed here. My mouth tries to form words to say this, and apologize.

"Come on." Blake takes my wrist and pulls my hand toward him.

"I can't."

"Ruby, look at me. You did that." He smiles like it hurts. His hold on my wrist is firm.

My fingers are clenched in my palm. "I wasn't . . . I don't . . ." How could I have been this stupid?

"Don't do this, Ruby." The heaviness of Blake's breath is filling the car. "All I need you to do is touch it."

"I . . . can't."

"You have to . . . do *something*." Still holding my wrist, Blake reaches around me with his other hand and holds the back of my head.

My mouth goes dry. If I don't touch him, will he make me do something worse?

Jaw tight, I force my fingers to curl around the base of his penis. They barely reach all the way around.

Blake almost chokes into my hair, "Good girl, Ruby."

Slowly I move my hand up the length. Before I get to the dark head and the glistening droplet—I can't touch that, I can't—I slide my hand back down. I never imagined flesh as hard as this. And I want to stop now.

"Come on, Ruby." Blake flicks his tongue into my ear. It feels so repulsive I can't believe I ever liked him doing it before. "I love you," he says, still holding my head, reminding me what he could make me do. If he does, I know I will vomit. I have never been this stupid in all my life.

Up the length of Blake's penis, I draw my fingers. The head, we were told in Health, is incredibly sensitive. It is also . . . my God . . . incredibly smooth. My hand smears the droplet. Smooth like a Chinese checker marble, and I like it, only—

It is spurting, hot and creamy, into my cupped hand. Blake is groaning against the side of my head. I want to push myself into the cold night air and run.

Blake reaches under the car seat. He hands me a box of kleenex.

I swipe at my hand, throw the wad of kleenex on the floor and take more, determined to rid every crease between my fingers and around my ring of any trace of Blake. Why does it have to occur to me that probably none of this would have happened to *Nan*?

Pressing myself against the passenger door, I swear I will not cry. Not here. Not now. I can hear Blake beside me tucking himself back into his pants, re-buckling his belt. Congratulating himself, probably, on a job well done.

"That wasn't so bad, Ruby, was it."

"Take me home."

Blake backs out of the laneway, guns the engine. The car leaps forward into the night. The skin of my hand is tight and sticky. I want to spit into it again and again and rub it on the car seat till I am clean. But my mouth is dry. And the seat of this car is probably as dirty as I am.

Along side streets, golden rectangles of light shine from houses. The car turns a corner. Streetlights and neon signs blur by.

"Pull over, please."

"Here?"

"Yes." I don't explain, and I don't care if Blake waits for me or not.

The gas attendant gives me the key. "Around the side," he tells me.

The washroom is a filthy little room, but there is water in the tap and soap in the dispenser, and that's all I need. For now.

When I open the door, the car is still there, blue and heavy under the bright lights of the gas station. I walk past it to the sidewalk. I hear the car door slam shut, but will not turn.

Blake shouts, "Let me take you home."

"I prefer to walk."

"You'll be late if I don't give you a ride."

"I know."

He runs to catch up with me. "Ruby, I thought you wanted . . . I thought when you asked . . ."

I will not admit to him, can hardly admit to myself, that I thought I wanted it too. My legs still feel wobbly as I walk away.

AT HOME, Mom is sitting in her chair in the living room, staring at the television. She should be in bed. She looks tired. And she is smoking. She didn't smoke for over a week after she came home, but tonight there are several butts in the ashtray beside her. Angry and scared, I want to snatch the cigarette from Mom's hand and slap it.

"Where have you been?"

"At the dance."

"Did Blake bring you home? I didn't hear his car."

Canned laughter from the television. I feel sick. I need a bath.

"No. I . . . We broke up."

Part of me wants to crawl up into Mom's lap like I haven't done since before Susie was born. I want her to rock me, stroke my face and tell me it's all okay.

"Well, Nan, there will be other boys."

"Don't . . . !" Inside me something explodes. "Don't call me that! *Please!*" Into my mother's shocked face I yell, "*Nan* is your little girl, so smart she could read before kindergarten. *Nan* is the little girl who never complained when you bought her ugly clothes. She drank Orange Crush and wanted to be a teacher because she knew it would make you happy. But it didn't, and I can tell you now that nothing I ever do will. *And . . .*" Tears stream down my face. "My name is *Ruby. Ruby,* Mother! Get it? My name is . . . Ruby!"

THE WATER IN THE TUB is as hot as I can stand it, and as deep as it can be. I lie back in it and cry. About what happened tonight, about Gramma, about Mom. It's about how much I want to see Daniel again, except he's probably dumped me. And Gramma can't die. How can I have been so stupid? I have to see Daniel again.

I cry until the water in the tub doesn't feel hot any more, then scrub every inch of my body.

And then I shower. When I'm done, the skin of my breasts, my thighs, my toes—all of me—is red. I bundle myself into clean flannel pyjamas. I can't wait to get into my bed.

In the doorway of his room, Gary is staring at me.

"Don't . . . say . . . anything."

"I just wanted . . . are you okay?"

I cannot answer him. What happened tonight with Blake I probably won't even be able to talk about to Patty. I have washed Blake off of me, but not my humiliation. Without speaking to Gary again, I close the door of my room behind me.

CHAPTER
SEVENTEEN

FOR THE NEXT FEW DAYS, everything at home is normal, or as normal as it ever is in my house. One day after school, though, when I go into the kitchen for a glass of milk, Mom is just standing there. Not making supper or wiping the counter, just standing, staring out the kitchen window. Softly but more tightly wound than I've ever heard her, she says, "Maybe I should just leave."

The motor in the refrigerator shudders into silence. My mother's words expand to fill the room but make no sense. Mothers don't leave. Except to pick up groceries or return library books or go have coffee with a neighbour. But that's what my mother said. *Maybe I should leave.* Leave home? Leave me? Because I'm not speaking to Gary? Because of what I did with Blake? Because I lost my temper when she called me Nan?

Mom turns from the window, looks right at me and says, "I just don't know if I can take any more."

This is not my mother speaking. If my mother is not herself, who is she, and why, and what might she do? Maybe she *will* leave.

The tightness in my chest squeezes up and out through my eyes in stupid tears that make no sense. Why should I care if she leaves? It's not as if I *need* her, meddling in my life, tossing out her little wizened gems of wisdom. But she shouldn't *want* to leave.

Mom seems suddenly to realize who I am, as if she's been somewhere far away and has just come back. "Don't cry. Stop. I shouldn't have said that."

I swipe at my face with my palms.

"I'm sorry," she whispers. "It's just . . . I didn't mean it." She reaches for a cigarette in the pack on the table, places it between her lips, and fumbles for her lighter. "I don't know what that was. I'm sorry." She flicks the ignitor several times before it lights. She draws smoke deep into her lungs and holds it there.

THAT NIGHT, AFTER SUPPER, Mom sends April and Susie away to play, and Dad tells me and Gary that Gramma has to go into hospital. They've stopped treatment, she's in a lot of pain now, and she's going to need a lot of care.

"Can't she come here?"

Mom stiffens at her end of the table, but I go on. "She can have my room. I'll sleep on the couch."

"Your mother and I discussed that possibility," Dad says carefully, "but she would find caring for Gramma so soon after her own surgery very difficult."

"I could help."

"I'd help too," Gary says.

"You both have school," Mom says. "She'll need help with . . . things you can't do."

"Like getting to the bathroom," Dad says.

The thought of Gramma so weak, so dependent, knocks me back in my chair. But, "I can take time off. Patty can bring me assignments. I can take Gramma to the bathroom for however long it takes till she's strong enough to get there herself again."

From inside her cloud of smoke, Mom is shaking her head.

"But wouldn't it be nicer for her to be able to get well here instead of in a hospital?"

Mom and Dad look at each other. Gary says, "I think she isn't going to get well, Ruby."

Why is it that any time he speaks to me lately, there's nothing for me to say?

Mom's lips wrap tightly around her cigarette. Dad's face admits the truth of what Gary said. I push myself away from the table and force my legs to carry me from the kitchen and down the hall.

On my bed I stretch out stiffly and stare at the ceiling. If Gramma dies, she will never again lie on this bed and talk with me. How can this be? She'll never take me shopping again either. I'll be stuck with Mom and whatever she thinks I should wear. And she'll never teach me bridge. Gramma was going to teach me how to play bridge.

I want her here with me now. I want her well, and sleeping over on our chesterfield like she sometimes did. Like nights she was coming up to the cottage with us the next day. And like the night after Poppa died.

In the morning that time, I crawled under her covers and nestled against her soft side. Her flowery smell was tinged with something sour. Mom had told me Poppa was in heaven with God now, but I wasn't sure I believed in heaven. I knew only that I'd never see Poppa again. We'd never do our card tricks together, or roast marshmallows over the candle after Christmas dinner. "Gramma," I asked her, "can people still see us when they're dead?"

"I believe they can. Yes."

"Do you believe in heaven and . . . and the other place?"

"Hell, you mean?"

"Don't let Mom hear you say that."

"Hell, why not?" Gramma chuckled.

Poppa was dead and Gramma *chuckled!*

"I do believe in heaven," she said, "and you know what else? I believe your Poppa is with us still, with everyone who loved him. In here, you know?" She patted her own heart, then mine. "My goodness," she exclaimed, "a bump."

I giggled.

Gramma slipped her hand over to the other side of my chest. "My goodness, another bump!" She wrapped her arm around me and gave me a strong hug. "Oh my, you're getting to be such a big girl."

Clutching my nubbly bedspread in my fist, I roll over onto my side, knowing I'll never be big enough not to need my gramma.

THE NEXT DAY, I overhear my parents talking in their bedroom.

"I can't do it, Ted. I can't."

"You mean you're going to just leave her there alone? Good God, Joan, she's your mother. You're her only child."

"That person hooked up to those tubes, those machines, is not my mother, she's not. I can't go back, and I don't want to hear any more about it."

Dad storms out of their room. I follow him to his workshop. Until I'm there among his tools and boards and sawdust, it doesn't occur to me that I never have been before. Probably no one has, not even Mom.

Now I don't know what to say. Dad looks at me, his fist clenched on his workbench. He shakes his head and looks away.

"I want to go see her, Dad."

"It's not a good idea," he says.

"Why?"

"You heard what your mother said. It would be very diffi-cult for you."

"I want to go, Dad. She's . . . she's *Gramma*."

Dad stares at the raw end of a board and nods. "Gary wants to go too."

IN THE CAR, no one talks. The details of the streets we travel to the hospital blur past as I think about what I might talk to Gramma about, depending on how she is, and if I get to spend some time with her alone. How I've been trying to reach Daniel. Does she know he called and Mom didn't tell me? I wonder if Gramma would tell me if she ever disap-proved of any of Mom's boyfriends. Could I ask Gramma outright about the man whose photo is in Mom's dresser?

The cars and buildings rushing past remind me, alone in the back seat behind Dad and Gary, of riding in the back seat of Gramma and Poppa's car when I was little, the time I was going to go downtown shopping with Gramma the next day, but first was sleeping over at their house. I sat up straight, I remember, with my pyjamas, toothbrush and clean under-wear in a brown paper bag on my lap. We didn't have any suitcases then; it was before we had the cottage. The white streetlights and coloured neon signs rushed together in a blur. Outside my grandparents' little house, garden smells hung chaotic and heavy in the night air. Blossoms on the snowball bush beside the driveway almost glowed in the dark. It was so dark I knew it must be very late. But not too late for a bath before bed, Gramma said. The smell of her soap as she sloshed the washcloth over my back was like her garden. And it was creamy-smooth. Not like the itchy soap at home. Between the sheets spread on the flowered chesterfield, I wrapped my arms around Gramma's neck, which smelled like her soap, and she kissed me goodnight.

Dad parks the car across from the hospital. How much will Gramma have changed, I wonder, since I saw her at my birthday? It's been over a month. Not that long a time usually. But she's sick enough now to have to be here, where the halls smell of stale bodies and disinfectants and . . . Does death have a smell? Is that why Mom couldn't come back?

Gramma is allowed only one visitor at a time. Dad's going to go first. I watch him enter the door just beyond where an old man is shuffling along in a thin bath robe, his hand on the wall.

I know but don't know what I will find beyond that door. Gramma, of course, lying in a bed. But not like I found her in bed that morning years ago, when I woke her up to see if it was time to go downtown yet. Her face then rested soft and full against her pillow. Dad warns me she has lost more weight since I last saw her, and her hair has thinned too.

Something about the doorway to Gramma's hospital room both pulls and repels me. I want to see her. I have to.

But what if, like my mother, I am unable to take what's
beyond that door? What if, in this way, I am the same as her?
And if I'm like her in this way, how else?

"You scared?" Gary asks.

"A bit."

"Me too."

It's not a lot to have said, but I almost want to thank him,
and would except Dad is coming out of Gramma's room
already.

"She's barely conscious," he says. "Are you two sure you
want to do this?"

We both nod. Gary says, "You go ahead if you want."

I ask Dad if she's in pain.

"No. She's pretty heavily sedated. But don't stay too long."

If I had not just seen Dad come out of this room, I would
not believe I was in the right one.

In the bed is a skeleton with greyish skin stretched over it.
Its mouth hangs open. Tubes come out of its nose and its
arm. Faster than I went into the room, I am out of it and in
Dad's arms, shaking.

After a minute Gary says, "Can we just go home now,
Dad?"

"You've changed your mind about going in?"

"If Ruby can't take it . . . I don't have half the guts she has."

Still clinging to Dad, I look at Gary, who's clearly shaken.
Guts? Me?

CHAPTER
EIGHTEEN

IT'S HARD TO GET that hospital image of Gramma out of my head. Each day at school, for the rest of the week, I keep expecting to be called down to the office for the phone call telling me she's gone. Friday after school, I'm peeling potatoes and trying to remember the conversation I had with Daniel, so long ago it seems now, about peeling potatoes and being happy. I try to calculate how many potatoes I've peeled since Mom started saddling me with the job, and how many she must have peeled before that. Is that what she couldn't take any more that day she went weird? Mom and Susie, I realize, are arguing in the living room.

"I wasn't," Susie says.

"I saw you."

"You didn't! It wasn't me."

Curls of potato peel fall into the kitchen sink.

"Susie, I cannot believe you would lie to me—and so *blatantly*."

"Even if I *was* breaking ice," Susie yells, "*so . . . what!?*"

"Go to your room."

Susie storms through the kitchen. So many times I've wished Mom would for once find some fault with perfect little Susie, and now she has. I never thought it would feel awful.

What is it with Mom anyway? Like Susie said, so what if she *was* breaking ice on her way home from school?

I scoop the peels into the garbage, cover the potatoes in the pot with cold water, flick on the element underneath them, and rinse my hands.

Mom is still standing at the living room window and staring out. The grey in her hair is noticeable. I go stand behind her and look out the window too, trying to see what she sees in the bubbles of thin white ice in the hard black puddles.

Some of the bubbles are shattered. I hear the satisfying cracking and crunching as my own feet have pressed, every fall and winter, on the fragile crystal layers. Susie likes doing it too, I guess, breaking that thin cold layer on top to get at what's underneath. Is that what Mom is so upset about? The possibility that Susie could become more like me?

Mom's shoulders are heavy, her arms wrapped around herself as if she's cold. It's almost like she's afraid of something.

She is, of course. She's afraid of Gramma dying.

I want—the impulse startles me—to reach out and touch her. To tell her, *Don't be scared, it's all right.*

But is it? How can it be when your mother is dying and when love is trapped inside you, like bubbles beneath brittle ice.

The metallic tap-tap of the lid on the potatoes rattles in the kitchen. I go to turn down the heat. Mom passes me and goes down the hall to the bathroom. Then Dad comes home.

"Hi Ruby. How are you doing?"

I shrug. "All right."

"How's your mother?"

"I don't know." I put the lid back on the pot. "Why?"

"She didn't tell you?"

"What?"

"Gramma . . ." He sighs. "Just after noon."

I can't believe Mom didn't tell me. But I guess she just couldn't.

I go to my room and fall face down on my bed. I should have gone back into Gramma's room that day. I had a chance to say goodbye, but I blew it. I try to think of Gramma being in heaven, in heaven with Poppa. It doesn't help. I need her here. No one in the world understands me like she does, always knows the right thing to say.

Like she *did. Knew.*

I roll over on my back and try to remember the things she said to me after Poppa died. I replay it all in my mind. Waking up to find her sleeping on our chesterfield, the sour smell of her neck, every word she said. When I come to the moment she hugged me and said I was getting to be such a big girl, tears trickle, finally, into my ears and pillow. I roll over again and nuzzle my wet face into my bedspread. *What am I going to do, Gramma? I need you.* I clamp my teeth down on my bedspread and cry. Because she is gone. And because I should have made myself go back to see her. To be with her. But I didn't. After all the times she was there for me. Was *anybody* there with Gramma when she died?

My ribs hurt from crying. I curl up, pull the covers over top of me, and cry some more.

"Nan?"

My eyes feel hot and swollen. Mom is standing in the doorway of my room.

"Time to come have supper."

Is she talking about having supper? Like it's any other day and Gramma isn't dead?

"I'm not hungry."

She takes a step into my room and reaches toward me, almost places a hand on my shoulder. "You have to eat, Nan," she says. "Come on. Before it gets cold."

Her mother died today. And she didn't go back either. I guess the least I can do is not argue.

AS MOM DISHES SUPPER onto our plates and sets them on the table, it strikes me there's something wrong with the way she is moving. No. What's wrong is how normally, for her, she is behaving. Spooning vegetables, sitting down, lifting her fork to her mouth, the same way she always does.

Around the table no one speaks. The sound of the forks on the plates, even Dad's chewing, feels loud. The radio, for once, is not on for the news. Gramma has died. What else could anyone need to know?

The fact of my empty plate surprises me. I have eaten every chunk of potato, every stick of carrot, the entire slice of meatloaf Mom gave me. When she offers a second helping, I take more. I dump a blob of ketchup in the middle of my plate and mash my meatloaf into it, not understanding how I can eat at all, never mind be ravenous.

When my plate is again empty, I ask, "When will the funeral be?"

Mom holds her lighter to her cigarette.

Dad answers. "Tuesday."

The end of Mom's cigarette glows red. "You don't have to go." She snaps shut her lighter.

"I . . ." Something squeezes tight inside my chest. "I want to."

"It's not a good idea."

"Are you saying . . . ? Are you saying I *can't* go?"

Mom picks a fleck of tobacco from her lip. "You know what happened when you went to see her."

"That's not the same. I . . ." I can't believe she would throw that up at me.

"A funeral is not a pleasant experience. And Lord knows there will be plenty of others for you to go to when you're older." Smoke curls around Mom's hand and face.

My hands grip the sides of my plate. I imagine myself lifting it and smashing it to the floor.

"Joan . . ." Dad puts down his fork and pushes back his chair. He comes to stand behind me and rests his hands on my shoulders. "Ruby is old enough—now—to go to her grandmother's funeral."

CHAPTER
NINETEEN

THE DAY BEFORE THE FUNERAL is one of those late fall days when it should be raining or even snowing, but the sun is shining down hard on the knots of kids standing around outside the school. A car with a noisy muffler roars into the parking lot. Blake and some red-head.

This is not a world I can be part of today. The colours and edges of everything outside my own bubble of reality are too sharp and too loud.

"Patty? Would you tell Mrs. Moffatt about my grand-mother?"

Patty looks at me sympathetically. "Sure, Ruby. You don't think you can tell her yourself?"

"It's not that. I don't want anyone at school calling home."

"Why would they?"

"'Cause I won't be here. There's something I have to do today. Cover for me? Please?" I hand Patty my books. "You

don't have to lie for me or anything. Just say, you know . . .
my grandmother died." It's still so weird to say those words.
The bigness of what they mean.

Patty and I agree to meet up again at the time I should be
getting out of school, and I cross the street to the bus stop.

After Poppa died, I remember, I went by myself to the
basement and dug a candle out of the Christmas box. I
found some matches and half a bag of marshmallows in a
kitchen cupboard and took them to my room. Quietly, by
myself and with my door closed, I roasted one marshmallow
over the Christmas candle, and saying goodbye to Poppa, I
ate it.

Today I'm going downtown to where Gramma worked
and where she took me shopping when I was little. Except
for the day I left school early after yelling 'nipples' in the hall,
I've never skipped classes before, and it feels like everyone
on the bus is looking at me. I've never been downtown by
myself before either. When the bus pulls into the subway
station, I follow everyone down the stairs and head for the
westbound platform. West to Yonge I have to go, then south.

On the subway, the wheels of the train clack along the
rails in time to my heartbeat, just like they did when I went
downtown with Gramma. Back then, my feet dangled off
the edge of the seat, and the big pink flowers on Gramma's
dress bumped against my grey pleated skirt. Today a
stranger smelling of garlic sits beside me.

At the entrance to the store, I stop. Lights sparkle all through the perfume department. Familiar music slows the movements of shoppers. It dawns on me suddenly that it's Christmas music. Christmas is only a couple of weeks away. How did I not notice?

And what is it I thought I was going to do here? This is, after all, just a store. Someone jostles my arm. "Excuse me."

Rather than blocking the aisle as I gawk, I start to wander. Fast through the perfumes, sharp and overpowering. Nothing like Gramma smelled, flowery and pink. I wander through purses and belts, through women's clothing, then decide to ride the *excalators*, as Gramma called them, to children's wear.

There aren't nearly as many dresses for little girls as there used to be, and most of them are muddy-coloured compared to the ones Gramma and I looked at that day she brought me shopping here. I try to imagine which dress Gramma might buy me if I were shopping with her now, and was still little enough for these dresses.

But I'm not little. And she's not here.

I wish we had come shopping here way more. Did Mom stop letting Gramma bring me after the day she bought me that dress with the buttons in the back?

An older woman, holding the hand of a little girl, comes into the children's clothing department. I have to leave.

"Excuse me," I ask the saleswoman at the cash desk, "can you tell me where the washrooms are?"

She points over beyond the appliances. Did she know my gramma, I wonder?

I remember this narrow hallway behind the stoves and fridges, but a plaque with a picture of a lady on it has replaced the sign that used to say "Ladies." I remember that sign because Gramma was so proud I could read it, even though I was only in kindergarten. She was also proud when I passed with honours out of grade eight. I need her to still be proud of me, even if I haven't done anything very smart lately.

I miss her so much. How will I ever stop missing her?

The washroom is empty today, but it was crowded that day I was here with Gramma. It must have been a Saturday. When one of the cubicle doors opened, Gramma pushed me forward and said, "Wait for me out here by the sinks when you're done." Beside me, in the next cubicle, I heard a huge gush. I imagined an elephant sitting on the next toilet. There was, of course, no elephant in the row of ladies by the sinks when I came out. Among all of them putting on lipstick, brushing their hair and snapping shut purses, I sidled up to the flowered hips I thought were Gramma's. I splashed my hands quickly under the tap because the flowered hips were moving away. Without even making sure I was following, Gramma was leaving—without me! I burst into tears. Gramma appeared beside me immediately and dried my face. "Heavens to Betsy, girl, what's the matter?"

"Oh, Gramma!" I pointed to the exit, "I thought you'd left without me!"

Gramma really *has* left me now. I lean back against the concrete wall and try, myself, to dry the tears that seep out of me. But it seems they will never stop coming.

BY LUNCHTIME, I think about heading home or back to school. There doesn't seem much point in what I'm doing—wandering among things that remind me of being here with Gramma. But it would be weird to show up at school now, and I don't want to be at home.

In the cafeteria, I pick up a pot of tea that I can make last for as long as I want to sit, and find a table in the corner, away from most of the Christmas shoppers. It's impossible to think of Christmas without Gramma.

Usually I drink my tea clear, but decide today to fill half the cup with milk and dump in two packets of sugar the way Gramma did for me when I was little. It's surprising how much the sweet creamy taste makes it possible to imagine Gramma being here, as though she's just come to sit with me one more time. *Don't worry about me, Ruby. I've had a good life, and it will be good for me to see your poppa again. And don't worry about you either. You're a wonderful girl and you're going to be just fine.* The Gramma who lay on my bed with me at home is the one telling me these things. What she became near the end, I realize, hasn't entered my head all day.

By the time I've drained the last of my tea, there's only about half an hour to kill before leaving to hook up with Patty. I wander through gloves and scarves, candy, games and then toiletries.

So many kinds of soap, including, I realize—in a flush that comes right up through my body and into my chest—the pink soap Gramma always used. I hold a box of it close to my face. The flowery smell tickles my nose the same happy way the warm nubbly washcloth tickled my skin when Gramma gave me a bath. Everything I love about Gramma is in the smell of this soap. I have to stop myself from crying as I take three bars to the cash desk.

Back home, after collecting my books from Patty, I tuck one flowery pink bar in my shirt drawer. Another I tuck underneath my pillow. And one I put in a cupboard in the bathroom so no one will use it but me. Which I'll do tonight when I have a bath before bed.

THAT NIGHT, Mom and Dad are going to the funeral home to receive visitors. I offer to stay with my sisters so Gary can go too. But as soon as the car pulls out of the driveway, I send them to their room to play. Long after the car has disappeared, I stand at the window and stare at the spot by the hedge where Gramma would appear if she were coming to visit. I know she isn't. Not today. Not ever. But will I ever *really* know it?

Missing Gramma somehow makes me miss Daniel even more than I already did. Maybe, while Mom and Dad are out, I should try calling him again instead of waiting till next time I'm at Patty's, and I'll just suffer whatever consequences come when his number turns up on the bill.

I'll do it. Right now.

Spinning away from the window, I almost bump into April.

"Ruby, will you play with me?"

"Can't you go play with Susie?"

"She won't play with me any more."

"Well, I can't play with you right now either. Why don't you go colour in your colouring book?"

"Ruby, are you crying?"

"Just go, April—please?"

I can't call Daniel when I'm already such a mess. How did I even begin to think I could? I probably wouldn't get him anyway. I get a notepad and pen from the kitchen, and in the chair in the corner of the living room, tuck my feet underneath me.

Dear Daniel, I write.

I wish I could talk to you. I've tried to phone you but . . .

Should I mention the strange person who has sometimes answered?

. . . it seems you're never home when I do. I wish you would try phoning me again. For a long time I worried you weren't

calling because of what happened the time you hitchhiked down to see me, but I found out recently that you did call, at least once. Please phone me again if you can.

Remember me telling you about my gramma this summer? She died last week. I miss her. She always made me feel like it was okay to just be who I am, even when, sometimes, I'm not sure who that is. If I was old enough to go live by myself, I would want to go and live in my gramma's little house. When I think about being there with her, and my poppa too before he died, I feel like everything in my life will work out. It's hard at home, sometimes, to feel that way.

I miss you too, Daniel. I miss talking to you, and hugging you, and I miss how it felt whenever you touched me. Do you miss me?

I realize suddenly that I don't have Daniel's address. I won't be able to send what I'm writing. But somehow it feels hopeful just to have written him. I sign my note, *Love, Ruby.*

I fold the paper and realize April is on the floor beside me, colouring quietly in her Mickey Mouse colouring book. I didn't even hear her come in. I watch her not-quite-pudgy-any-more fingers curled around her crayon as she gives Mickey Mouse a purple face.

"Do you still want to play something, April?"

She nods.

"Just let me put this in my room first, okay?"

April gathers her crayons into her tin crayon box.

When I open the drawer of my dresser, the smell of Gramma's soap wafts out. I tuck my letter to Daniel near the back.

Passing my sisters' room, I poke my nose in. Susie is lying on her bed, reading.

"You okay, Susie?"

She looks up, shrugs and nods. I'm sure she's missing Gramma too, but I don't know how to talk to her. Although she has started to change a little lately, she can still make me feel like an idiot the way Mom does.

In the living room, April has spread her cut-out dolls across the coffee table.

"We have to get everybody dressed up," she says.

"Okay. Are they going to a party?"

"No, they're going to a *foonrle*."

"Oh."

We sort through the paper clothes and hook the tabs over the shoulders of the cardboard dolls as we find suitable outfits.

"Is Gramma in heaven now?" April asks.

"Do you think she is?"

"Yes." She looks up at me from the doll she is dressing. "Don't you?"

"If there is a heaven, then I'm sure Gramma is in it. But you know where I'm sure Gramma is—for sure?"

"Where?"

"In here." I put my hand over my heart.

April stares at it very hard.

"And she's in here too." I reach across the corner of the coffee table and place my hand on April's little chest.

April looks down, puts her hands over my hand, looks up at me and nods.

"Come here, you." I pull April toward me and hold her tight.

THE AFTERNOON OF THE FUNERAL, Patty's going to stay with Susie and April. While she's getting them busy with a game, Mom and Dad are whispering in the kitchen, Dad in his suit, Mom in her black dress. I'm thinking we'll have to leave soon if we're going to pick Gramma up on the way. And Gary should hurry up with the tie he has already reknotted about six times. I'm actually thinking Gramma should have stayed over last night so we could just all leave together from here, when it hits me again. Gramma is dead. It is, of course, her funeral everyone is dressed for so darkly.

WEAK LIGHT FROM THE STAINED GLASS windows seeps down over pews filled with people gathered to say goodbye to Margaret Lois Gibbons. Gramma. The never-ending patterns of coloured glass go right to the ceiling and comfort me in a funny way.

I asked Gramma once how what looked so dull outside could be so magically beautiful inside, and she said, "God works in mysterious ways." Then she winked so *I'd* know that *she* knew it wasn't really an answer, but that she didn't know how those stained glass windows worked either.

From the pulpit, the minister reads, "A time to mourn, and a time to dance . . . A time to keep silence, and a time to speak. A time to love, and a time to hate. A time of war, and a time of peace." The music of the Byrds' version that they still play on the radio starts up in my head.

I look across the rows of heads at Gramma's funeral, the men's bare and the women's covered, mostly in black or navy blue. My hat, light charcoal grey, Mom bought for me, I'm not sure when. But it's the first church hat I've had that wasn't white straw with a pastel-coloured ribbon.

"Please take out your hymn books and turn to Psalm Twenty-Three."

A shuffling of feet and papers.

"All rise."

Rain begins to beat upon the windows. The organist plays an opening chord.

Beside me Mom holds open the hymn book. "The Lord is my shepherd, I'll not want . . ." Her voice is strong. Like Gramma's, it occurs to me.

I sing too, but my voice is tight and thin. ". . . He lea-eadeth me, The qui-iet waters by."

After more shuffling and kneeling and bowing of heads, we stand for the next hymn. "What a friend we have in Jee-sus, All our sins and griefs to bear . . ."

Something cracks inside me. I cannot sing.

Mom's voice continues, strong, but beneath the hymn book her hands are shaking badly. Her eyes, though, remain dry. On top of my sadness, the sight of Mom resisting what she must be feeling seizes me, and tears spill down my face. How can she shake like this and still sing? "O-oh, what needless pain we su-uf-fer, Oh what needless pain we be-a-ar, All because . . ."

I want to unlock my throat and again join in the singing, for Gramma.

As the chords play for the next hymn, I take a deep breath and begin again. "God sees the little sparrow fall . . ."

I see the sparrow on the figurine Gramma gave me, and suddenly I can't do it. Sing. Even though Mom sings strong and clear. As her own mother lies dead in a box in front of us. And her hands tremble with . . .

With fear? Fear that she might cry?

She does not want me to see her cry.

Is that why she didn't want me at Gramma's funeral? She wanted to protect me from all this sadness, and still does? As if seeing someone else's sadness will make my own worse?

But so much worse than any grief is this awful trembling. I'd like to tell Mom it's okay, I'm okay. But maybe it's not just me she's holding it in for. Something, I don't know what, makes me think it's . . . herself. It's herself, maybe, that she's trying to protect by not crying.

Except that doesn't make any sense. Does it? I stare at her, wanting to say she doesn't have to do this, hold it all in, but she will not look at me.

So I reach out—I cannot bear those hands—and touch my mother's forearm. The smallness of it beneath my fingers surprises me.

Mom's voice, for the briefest second, is silent. Under the hymn book, her hand is shaking harder. But she takes it, carefully, and she places it over mine.

Together we get our voices back. Both our eyes are wet now, but with the rest of the congregation, we finish, "If God so loves the little sparrow . . ."

CHAPTER
TWENTY

AFTER DOING DISHES a few days later, when Dad is reading the paper in the living room and the girls and Gary have gone to their rooms, Mom says to me, "Sit down."

I sit, but can't think why I might be in trouble.

"I want to try to explain something . . . that . . . may be hard for you to understand."

Why she started smoking again? What she meant that day she threatened to leave? Has she forgotten that she has already in her own oblique way explained sex to me?

"I was . . . afraid for you."

Mom, I realize, is doing what for so long I have wanted. She is talking to me. About something real. But what?

"You seemed so crazy about him."

Suddenly this feels like a dangerous conversation to be having. I want, suddenly, to be somewhere else—anywhere else.

"Whenever you saw him," Mom continues, "it was like there was a light on inside you for hours afterwards."

Daniel. She is talking about Daniel.

"But you're only sixteen . . ."

I don't need to hear about being too young to know what's good for me. I'd get up from the table now, but something holds me.

"I'm not saying it was the right thing to do, just trying to explain . . ." Mom folds her hands on the table in front of her. "What I'm trying to say . . . is . . . I don't happen to think that boy was right for you, but . . ." She swallows. "I'm sorry I tried to keep him from you. I . . . shouldn't have done that."

"Was it because of the man whose picture is in your dresser?"

"I beg your pardon."

I shouldn't have mentioned him. I didn't know I was going to, but I don't know how—now—to pretend that I didn't.

"When I was getting your nightgown for you, when you were in hospital . . ." I've gone this far, what would it hurt if I just asked her? "Did you love him?"

Mom reaches for her pack of cigarettes. "I don't know what you're talking about."

"There was a photo of a man . . ."

She snaps closed the lid of her lighter. "The only man I have ever loved . . ." Smoke rises up her face. ". . . is your father."

This may be true. Or not. She is definitely wrong, though, about Daniel.

But she has said she is sorry.

And I don't want to fight.

Mom draws deeply again on her cigarette. Whether the man in her dresser was her Daniel or not—I have to accept—is hers to know, not mine.

"Mom . . . I'm sorry too."

She exhales, and when she sets down her cigarette, her eyes . . . they are like the eyes in that photo.

BEHIND GARY'S BEDROOM DOOR the radio is on low. *I was all right for a while, I could smi-ile for a while.*

I raise my hand and tap lightly.

But I saw you last night, you held my hand so tight . . .

I didn't see Daniel last night, but I tried calling him again, and this time—finally—he was the one to answer the phone.

Gary's door opens. On his desk are his weather maps and a notebook.

"Gary, I just wanted to say . . . you know that time . . . after I went out with . . . ?" I still can't say his name. "You were right."

Gary's jaw is tight. His eyes are sad. He nods.

"But I'm okay."

He pushes words from his mouth. "That's good." He stares at my face so hard I have to look away.

"Are you . . . ?" I make myself look at him again. "Are you thinking about being a weather man now or something, studying all these maps?"

"Maybe."

"Will Mom be happy about that, do you think?"

"No."

"So . . . how does the weather look?"

"Clearing." Gary manages something close to a smile. "It'll be clear for a few days."

It seems there should be something more to say, but I can't think what.

"Well, I'm going out now. See you."

Gary doesn't ask me where, but if he did I would tell him, Daniel is at his aunt's for the weekend, the one he stayed with when he was working at the Ex, and I am taking the bus and subway out to the west end to see him.

"Bye," Gary says.

In their bedroom, Susie and April are arguing about whether the cut-outs should go to a movie or to church. Downstairs, Dad is banging on something in his workshop. In the living room, Mom is standing at the window. Maybe some day we'll talk again. But today I am going to see Daniel, and it's like I have to work to keep my feet on the floor.

"Bye, Mom."

"Goodbye, Ruby. You have the fare you need to get back?"

"Yes." I close the vestibule door behind me and step out onto the porch.

In the sky, patches of blue are growing bigger. *Enough blue to make a pair of Dutchman's breeches,* Gramma used to say. On the sidewalk I turn and look back at my house.

Mom waves to me from the window, blowing smoke against the pane.

ACKNOWLEDGEMENTS

A number of people read parts or all of this story at various stages and helped it become what it is. For their input and encouragement I owe thanks to Teresa Toten, Sarah Ellis, Ann Goldring, Lena Coakley, Paula Wing, Hadley Dyer, Wendy Lewis, Kelly Stinson, Peter Carver, Barbara Greenwood, Loris Lesynski, Susan Adach, Nancy Hartry, Leona Trainer, Barbara Berson and Alison Millar.

An earlier version of a scene in *Becoming Ruby* was previously published as a postcard story—*Cream Soda*—in *grain* magazine, volume 28, number 2.